ROOKIE MOVES

A Checkmate Inc. Novel

Shelly Alexander

Copyright 2017 by Shelly Alexander
A Touch of Sass, LLC

All rights reserved. No part of this publication may be reproduced, distributed, or transmitted in any form or by any means, including photocopying, recording, or other electronic or mechanical methods, without the prior written permission of the publisher, except in the case of brief quotations embodied in critical reviews and certain other noncommercial uses permitted by copyright law.

This book is a work of fiction. All names, characters, locations, and incidents are products of the author's imagination. Any resemblance to actual persons living or dead, things, locales, or events is entirely coincidental.

Cover design by Wax Creative Designs

ISBN: 978-0-9979623-1-4

ALSO BY

SHELLY ALEXANDER

Shelly's sweeter titles (with a touch of steam):

The Red River Valley Series
It's In His Heart
It's In His Touch
It's In His Smile
It's In His Arms

Shelly's sizzling titles (with a lot of steam):

The Checkmate Inc. Series
ForePlay
Rookie Moves
Sinful Games (Coming Summer 2017)

About the Checkmate Inc. Series

Leo Foxx, Dex Moore, and Oz Strong spent their youths studying a chessboard, textbooks… and women, from afar. Now they're players in the city that never sleeps. Gone are their shy demeanors, replaced with muscle, style, and enough sex appeal to charm women of all ages, shapes, and cup sizes. They've got it all, including a multimillion-dollar business called Checkmate Inc.—a company they founded together right out of college.

Some guys are late bloomers, but once they hit their stride, they make up for lost time.

A fun, flirty, and dirty contemporary series in which the sizzling hot players of Checkmate Inc. meet their matches.

Dedication

For all the ladies out there that had big brothers looking out for them. They meant well. Really, they did.

And as always, for my husband. Thank you for the best 25 years of my life. I'm looking forward to at least 25 more.

Prologue

"Rookie? She'll be an expert when I'm done teaching her."
—Dex Moore

Let me share a little secret. Smart guys make the best lovers.

Why, you ask? Plain and simple: we work harder for it. Ever heard the phrase *curiosity killed the cat?* Well, if that were true, anyone with an IQ over 140 would be dead, including me. Let me assure you, I'm alive and well and living the dream.

You see, a high IQ often leads to curiosity and a desire to learn as much as possible. That's how we humans managed to land a man on the moon, discover antibiotics, and invent social media. That innate curiosity also makes us smart guys want to unlock the mysteries of women. I mean, women are the most fascinating and complicated species on the planet, right? So when we meet a woman that piques our interest, it drives our curiosity to soaring heights.

We want to study her. Figure her out. And if a guy is not only smart but also savvy, he'll want to find the key that unlocks her mind-blowing, roof-raising orgasms.

Lucky son-of-a-bitch that I am, I've built a kick-ass career on this very concept. Okay, my job isn't really built on the orgasm part. But Checkmate Inc. is definitely successful because we focus on the *whole* man and helping him transform into a better partner. In my humble opinion, a big part of being a better partner is making sure the lady is satisfied between the sheets.

Soooo. High IQ, curiosity, women, orgasms...see the connection? Seems so common sense to me. Then again, the word *obtuse* has been used to describe me more than once. That's right. I, Dexter Moore, was a certified chess team nerd back in the day. Deep down, I still am. Probably always will be. But you'd never know it from the muscle I've packed on at the gym, the sharp wardrobe I own, and the magazine covers I've graced with my business partners.

As a founding partner of a company that's grown into a multimillion-dollar business, I'm a quasi-celebrity, and I'm not quite thirty years old. It's a role I never expected when my college buddy convinced me to turn down a tech job on the West Coast to start Checkmate Inc. in the heart of Manhattan. Leo Foxx was the brainchild behind the company, but opening the retail arm was my idea. Now that we're expanding our retail studios into Europe and Dubai, I've somehow been labeled the jet-setting playboy out of all three Checkmate partners.

Although it's not exactly the image Checkmate wants, I don't mind the smoke screen. I can't commit to a serious relationship while I trot around the globe to oversee our expansion, a venture that could bankrupt Checkmate if I don't keep my eye on the prize.

Besides, the only woman I'd like to study and unlock so I can hear her ear-splitting cry of ecstasy as I fuck her to the edge of heaven is the one woman I can't have. And since she's one of my closest friends and my business partner's sister, a jet-setting playboy image is the perfect facade to hide my true feelings.

Chapter One

"Why do I find it so sexy when a guy says 'fuck?'" Ava's voice is the first thing I hear when I blow through the front door of her brother's Upper West Side apartment for her twenty-fifth birthday party.

"Hey, man," Leo says as I shuck my overcoat and hand it to him. His hair is the same dark blonde as Ava's, and they look so much alike that it still startles me after all these years. "Business meeting first thing Monday so you can bring me and Oz up to speed." Since Leo is Checkmate's CEO, he's always thinking of business. His new fiancée calls his name from the kitchen. "Welcome home. Glad you made it." He nods in the direction of his sister's voice. "It'll mean a lot to her." Leo disappears with my overcoat.

I'm jetlagged from traveling across more time zones than I can count, but I haven't missed Ava's birthday since I met her eight years ago. I follow that fearless voice and weave through the small crowd of guests.

"Seriously." Her voice rings with humor and wit. "Is it *normal* to think a guy saying 'fuck' is hot?"

I want to shout *fuck, fuck, fuck* at the top of my lungs. My hand tightens around the bouquet of long-stem roses I picked up on the way from the airport.

She's facing the wall of glass that looks out over Central Park, and the lights of Manhattan twinkle in the distance. The circle of guests gathered around her chuckle at her brazenness, and I smile as I walk up behind her. I love that about her too. She's bold, bodacious, and ridiculously out of bounds sometimes.

It's such a turn on.

I can barely control the urge to wrap my arms around her from behind and leave no space at all between us. I'd love nothing more than to feel that black clingy dress she's wearing slide against my expensive Italian dress pants, her ass against my crotch. The red fuck-me stilettos with straps that wrap around her slender ankles would put her perfect, round ass right about level with my crotch, even though I'm over six-feet. I'd run a hand up her half-bared thigh until the mini-dress was hiked around her waist and my fingers were buried in her—

"Dex!" Ava catches my reflection in the window and spins around. "You made it."

Fucking hell. I realize my jaw is hanging open, and I'm about to drool.

I swipe the back of one hand over my lips. "Uh," I manage to say. Really? Being the sharp-dressed playboy I supposedly am with an exceptional IQ and all, *uh* is the best I can come up with?

My eyes slide shut just long enough for her to throw both arms around my neck and kiss me on the cheek. I stiffen because that's become my automatic reaction to Ava. Every goddamn part of my anatomy goes rock-hard when I'm with her.

She hugs me tight. "I thought you were still in Dubai."

I'm *supposed* to be in Dubai. I cut my trip short and hopped a flight just to be here with her. "I wrapped things up early." I can't stop myself. I turn my face into her honey blonde hair and breathe her in. Her perfume is sweet and seductive, and it envelopes me until she breaks our embrace and takes a step back. "I just landed and picked these up on the way." I hold up the flowers.

I specifically bought yellow roses because they're the symbol of friendship, or so said the florist who might as well have robbed me at gunpoint. The cost of twenty-five roses is almost as much as the set of bangle bracelets I bought for Ava in Dubai's gold market.

I brush one hand down the front of my black custom suit jacket where the velvet box is nestled in the inside pocket. Ava is worth every cent and so much more. I can't put a price tag on the kind of friendship we have. How important she's become.

Even if I can't tell her. Ever.

Which sucks balls.

"They're beautiful." She takes the bouquet and fingers a yellow petal. The tips of her long, slender fingers glide over the silky flowers. One smooth mound, then another.

My balls tighten. My mouth starts to water again, and I clamp it shut so none will escape. Yes, drooling is another response that is beyond my control when I'm with her. My best friend's kid sister. The girl I've helped look after since she was a teenager. The girl I swore to protect from douchebags. I want her.

Ava Foxx isn't a flat-chested kid anymore. She's grown into a beautiful woman who turns heads when she walks into a room. Which drives me batshit crazy because I don't want other men undressing her with their beady eyes or fantasizing over her amazing body.

I want dibs on both.

Not going to happen, though. I can't break the promise I made to her brother. Leo has tried to shelter her since they lost their parents in a car accident eight years ago. My buddy may be the only man on the planet who hasn't noticed Ava is all grown up now, but hey, I can't fault him for that. I admire his fatherly overprotectiveness because I never experienced it from my own dad.

"Happy birthday, Rookie," I say low enough so only she can hear.

Her vivid blue eyes light up, and a sentimental smile plays at her lips. Happens every time I call her by the nickname I gave her a long time ago. It's something we share with no one but each other, and that makes my heart thump against my chest. I like knowing I have a part of her that no one else has, even if it's something as silly as a nickname.

She steps to my side and hooks an arm through mine.

"Everyone has met Dex, right?" she says to the group of friends standing in front of us.

They're watching with curious expressions. The four young women who are partners in Ava's up-and-coming web design agency called 5 Muse Designs are part of the small gathering. Vi lifts a brow. Bella raises a cocktail glass to her lips and lets it hover there without taking a drink as she stares at us. Peyton clears her throat, but everyone seems too mesmerized by my interaction with Ava to notice. Only Sophie seems oblivious. She's the programmer at 5 Muse and the gear-head in her makes her as obtuse as me.

I realize I've let the player smoke screen vanish, and I'm wearing my heart on my forty-five hundred dollar sleeve.

No way am I giving Ava the rest of her birthday present now. The bracelets are pretty flashy, so I'll wait until we're alone.

I glance around the crowd. "Hi." Another highly intelligent response from yours truly.

Everyone returns the greeting.

Gerard emerges from the dining room with his husband, Magnus, right on his heels. As always, they're dressed razor-sharp, and their slightly graying hair gives them a distinguished and wise look. "*Dexter, daaaaling,*" Gerard says. They fly in my direction with both hands extended. Not to shake mine, mind you. Instead, they take turns grasping my shoulders and kissing both of my cheeks.

I stole this couple away from the fashion scene in Milan when we opened the retail arm of Checkmate. After years in Italy, they like to think of themselves as European. Gerard's West Virginia accent is barely noticeable anymore.

"So glad you're back," Magnus says. "You look exhausted, Dexter."

Since they train and manage all of Checkmate's life-stylists, and I'm in charge of Checkmate's retail studios, they both report to me. Truth is, they saved my ass. I mean, a straight guy—whose typical daily wardrobe included a Columbia University sweatshirt, white socks, and flip flops—wanting to open a chain of high-end clothing stores for men? Come on. After Leo and

Oz finally stopped laughing and agreed to the venture, it took me all of thirty seconds to figure out I was in over my head.

Magnus and Gerard pull me toward the kitchen, one on each side. Each step leeches away the warmth I feel in Ava's presence. As I leave her, coldness settles over me, even though Leo's apartment is warm and cozy.

When I step into the kitchen, Leo has donned an apron and is helping his new fiancée, Chloe, prepare more food.

"Hey, Dex!" Chloe says, then holds out an open palm in front of Leo. "Told you he'd make it. Twenty bucks. Cough it up."

I've only known Chloe a month and a half, and she can already read me too well. Her woman's intuition could be dangerous. I absolutely do not want Leo to find out how I really feel about his sister.

Oz descends on me with a slap on the back. "You're here." Another brilliant deduction by a super smart guy. "You came all this way for free food and booze? You're such a damn cheapskate," Oz says like the hard-nosed smartass he pretends to be.

Okay, so the smartass part is right on target. But underneath the harsh exterior, he's really a great friend with a heart of gold, and he does a kick-ass job with Checkmate's research and development, so our products are always new, fresh, and cutting edge.

The three of us have been friends since our punk-ass college days on the chess team. We've come a long way since then, trading in our khaki team uniforms for expensive wardrobes. The only outward evidence that we were geeksters in our former lives is the glasses. We made a pact never to lose the glasses. Everything else that telegraphed 'nerd' is history. Even the casual jeans Leo and Oz wear nearly every day cost as much as a fucking Fiat.

I walk around the white granite and chrome island to give Chloe a kiss on the cheek. "You look great. Vacationing in

Russia was good to you."

She angles her cheek while cutting a stalk of celery into sticks.

"Sure you still want to marry this riffraff?" I nod to Leo. "I have better taste in clothes, and I drive a faster car."

"Watch it, asshole." Leo fans out the celery sticks on the tray. "I can still kick your ass."

I lift both brows and point at his apron, which sports a picture of our favorite chess piece—the horse—and says *Knight of the Kitchen*. "Right. You're a badass."

Oz belly laughs.

"The Bolshoi was a spectacular engagement present from Leo." She smiles at him and dishes up more finger foods. "I didn't know we were going until we got to the airport. It was incredible, and he was a champ about the whole thing."

"I don't know, man." Leo shakes his head. "The whole dudes-frolicking-in-tights thing was disturbing." He tries to mask a shudder but doesn't quite succeed. "Especially since we were sitting in the front row."

When Magnus and Gerard both sniff and cross their arms, Leo says, "No offense. It's just not my idea of sexy."

I laugh and snag an hors d'oeuvre from Chloe's tray. She swats at my hand.

"I almost forgot." Oz pulls out his phone and taps the screen.

My pocket dings.

"I'm sending you a number." Oz takes a sip of his beer. "Remember Cynthia Ethridge?"

How could I forget? I dated Cynthia several months ago. It was short lived but lasted long enough for our picture to show up in every gossip mag in the city. Turns out, Cynthia forgot to mention she had a husband tucked away on Long Island.

Oz still hasn't let me live that one down.

He gives me an evil grin. I swear, I'm going to crush him into dust the next time we play chess.

I narrow my eyes at him. "What about her?" I'm sure I'm going to regret the question.

"I bumped into her the other day." Oz takes another long, lazy drink like he's enjoying this. "Wanted me to tell you hi since you've changed your number and she can't reach you herself. She gave me her cell in case you've *misplaced* it."

Right. Misplaced. "File thirteen." That's code for *trash*. I deleted Cynthia's number about thirty seconds after I found out she was married. "I can find plenty of *single* women to date."

"Blow up dolls don't count." Oz reaches for Chloe's plate, and she cuts him down with a laser stare. He blanches and draws back an empty hand, at which point, Oz turns his smartassery back on me. "Regardless of what the gossip columns say, I know you haven't been out with a woman in a while. Are you sure you're not gay?" He makes a sweeping motion to indicate my attire. "I mean, you did take to the whole metro-stylish look like a duck takes to water." Oz hitches his chin at Magnus and Gerard. "What do you guys think?"

They look me up and down. And that's not the least bit awkward since they're a married gay couple, and I'm straight as a fucking arrow.

Gerard shakes his head. "Not registering on my gay-dar." He looks at his husband, who has one arm crossed over his chest and is tapping his jaw with the other hand as he studies me. "You?"

Finally, Magnus shakes his head. "Straight." He sighs like it's a shame, and he and Gerard wander into the dining room to join the fray of guests. And probably to polish off the rest of the champagne. Gerard *is* from Appalachian moonshine country, even if he acts European. Ish.

I take out my phone and delete the contact info Oz just texted to me. "Oops. I'm pretty bad about misplacing things these days."

"That's why you need an assistant," Leo says. "I'm tired of both of you using mine. She has too much on her plate."

My longtime assistant moved to California a few months ago, and I've yet to replace her. Oz, on the other hand, chews them up and spits them out like gum.

"I'm not going to be around enough to need an assistant of my own," I say.

Both of my business partners frown at me. Chloe stops chopping some sort of unrecognizable vegetable and gives me a soft look.

"That's what we need to discuss during Monday morning's business meeting. During the expansion, I may have to be on-site more than we'd planned." I reach for another hors d'oeuvre now that Chloe's look seems more sympathetic.

She slides the plate in my direction.

"You're still going to need an assistant." Leo shrugs. "So we hire someone who can travel with you."

I've got enough to worry about. I don't want an assistant tagging along. Maybe after things settle down, I can hire someone, but not until I figure out what the hell I'm doing overseas. Until then, I've worked out a plan with Leo's assistant. It's called email, telephone, and Skype—pretty cool inventions. And it'll be fine. I just have to nip Leo's determined look in the bud before it takes root and grows into an oak tree. When he gets an idea in his head, he won't let it go until the rest of us surrender. That's how I ended up on the cover of GQ instead of *Technology Today*.

It's also the reason my parents disowned me.

"No assistant right now." I shake my head.

Leo ignores me. "I'll have Human Resources start interviewing applicants." He pops a carrot into his mouth and chomps. "Maybe we should hire a guy instead of a woman." Ava walks in, holding an empty platter at the same moment Leo says, "Otherwise, you'll end up fucking her."

Ava stops cold and stares at her brother, then at me. The brightness in her eyes dims. It's hardly noticeable, but I notice everything about Ava.

Oz laughs. "Dex fucking his assistant," he says to Chloe, since she's our public relations account rep. "Now there's a PR nightmare for you."

Ava's eyes simmer, and her face flushes. Just barely, but I've come to learn every movement, every gesture, every miniscule flash of emotion in her expression, and I know this bothers her.

No one else seems to notice that Ava's usual grand entrance has been replaced with silence.

And they call *me* obtuse.

An ache starts deep in my chest, but my chest expands at the same time because of what I hope this means. Her feelings for me might go deeper than friendship. And doesn't that make me frontrunner for Asshole of the Year? I mean, really. I deserve a trophy or something, because no matter how we might feel about each other, I can't go there. But I don't like the look of disappointment on her face, and I want to do something... anything to wipe it away.

Truth is, I know exactly what I want to do to her. I want to take her in my arms and kiss her. I want to peel that goddamn dress off of her and fuck her to the edge of heaven. All night long.

Since that's not possible, I scramble to salvage the situation some other way. "I don't want any attachments while I'm working on the expansion, so I won't be fucking anybody for a while."

The shade of Ava's face deepens to scarlet.

Shit.

She's so still, she could be carved from marble. She's a work of art, more beautiful than any of the famous pieces I see in the museums around Europe when I travel there for business.

I'm a founding partner of a cutting-edge company that has made me filthy rich. I have a kick-ass apartment not far from here with a killer view. I've been labeled a drop-dead gorgeous player in the city that never sleeps. All things that can get me laid any night of the week and much more than twice on Sunday. So why does it suck so goddamn hard to be me right now?

Chapter Two

I ease into the living room and pour myself a Macallan neat from the wet bar. I escape the crowd by hiding in the corner shadows of Leo's expansive balcony while I sip the rich whisky. The late autumn air is crisp and cold, and it prickles my skin. The bustling city noises from below drift up to meet me as I take in the magnificence of the Manhattan skyline at night.

It's a far cry from where I grew up. Princeton, New Jersey's small college town charm, where both of my parents are professors, is a different world, and my childhood seems like another lifetime.

I love a party as much as the next guy. And since I'm friendly, outgoing, and usually dressed to kill—or at least maim—New York City's liveliness is my gig. But I'm not in a party mood after seeing the hurt in Ava's eyes.

I brace my forearms against the railing, roll the fine single malt scotch around in my glass, and brood.

Suddenly, unexpectedly, I have a yearning to go home to New Jersey. A pull deep in my chest to see my parents and the home where I grew up. Only I've been there and done that. Tried to reach out to them and reestablish contact after they cut me off for "wasting my gifted mind on Leo's hair-brained folly."

I blow out a smirk and take another drink. Even my intellectual parents, who put academics above all else, can't deny that Checkmate Inc. turned out to be anything but foolishness. A company that started with biologically engineered cologne for men that is specifically designed to produce supercharged pheromone production in women has to be the most brilliant stupid idea on the planet.

Sort of like Teenage Mutant Ninja Turtles.

Who knew it would be a worldwide success, right?

Leo, Oz, and I managed to turn that *pathetic idea*, as my

parents called it, into what will soon be a worldwide chain that makes truckloads of money.

The balcony door slides open behind me, and heels click against the tile. I don't turn around because I know it's Ava. I have this super power to detect her presence. It wraps around me like a soft, velvety blanket. It warms me from the inside out, just like the Macallan.

It doesn't hurt that her personality is bigger than the Empire State Building, and she's impossible to ignore.

I hear her fingers slide across the patio table as she walks past it. "Hey." She eases up to the railing and stands so close that her perfume makes my brain stutter and my dick twitch.

"Hey, Rookie." I take another drink.

I can sense her smile through the darkness.

She's got Leo and Chloe's little dog tucked under one arm, and he whines. I scratch Toby's tiny head. He strains toward me and almost wiggles out of Ava's grasp.

"Whoa." I grab him because the thought of the little guy shooting over the balcony makes me nauseous. "I think he's safer inside." I set my glass on the table, crack the door just enough so he can fit through, and slide it shut again. He presses his little wet nose against the glass and looks up at me. "Sorry, buddy." I kneel down and talk to him through the glass like he can hear. "Can't let anything happen to you." His tongue lolls to one side, and he turns and trots away.

"You think my party's lame," Ava blurts.

I grab my drink and rejoin her at the railing, with my forehead crinkled. No idea what she's talking about. "What makes you say that?"

I'm facing her, looking down at her. She lifts her gaze to mine, and the distant city lights cast a glow across her flawless face.

"Well, you're out here alone for one." Her breath caresses my jaw and neck.

Goddamn, I want to kiss her. I want to lift her against the wall right here and now and fuck her until her screams of pleasure shatter every window in the building. I've wondered what she'd look like in the throes of an all-out, mind-blowing orgasm. Dreamed of it. Fantasized about it.

But I can't get sideways with my business partner over his sister. Not with Checkmate's expansion at stake. It could ruin us. And I'm one hundred and fifty percent certain Leo wouldn't appreciate either having to replace all that glass or me fucking his sister. Especially since he regularly makes Oz and I renew our vow to cut the balls off any douchebag who tries to make a move on his baby sister.

His words, not mine. I often wonder if Leo has actually looked at his little sister lately. It's pretty apparent to anyone with eyesight that she's not a baby. My stare brushes over her mouth-watering cleavage. Nor is she little.

"I needed a minute alone." My voice is gravelly. Hopefully, I sound tired and not sexually frustrated. Truth is, I'm so fucking both. I'm tired and sexually frustrated from not being able to have the woman I want. "Jet lag is a bitch." Still facing her, I lean against the railing again. "Plus Leo and Oz can be dicks sometimes."

"Not wanting you to fuck the help is kind of dick-ish," Ava deadpans. She takes my drink from my hand without asking and sips it.

She's probably the only person who can get away with that. She can drink from my glass, eat from my plate, lick anything from my—

She takes another sip and traces her lips with the tip of her tongue as she sets the glass on the railing. "Maybe this will warm me up. It's cold out." She shivers and rubs her arms with both hands.

In a flash, I've shucked my jacket, and I drape it around her shoulders.

"Thank you." She snuggles into it. "What you said in there…

you know..." She takes another sip, then pulls a plump bottom lip between her teeth like she's nervous. "If you stop sleeping around, New York's gossip rags might go out of business. You've been their favorite bachelor for a few years now."

"It's called gossip for a reason. My image is blown way out of proportion." I gotta be honest, though. A few years ago when my mind, my heart, and my prick started to notice Ava as a woman, I tried to fuck her out of my system by shagging a different woman every weekend. I was a perfect gentleman about it and never tried to hide my aversion to long-term commitment. Every woman I was with went in with her eyes wide open. That fuck-athon lasted about six months, but the reputation stuck, and I'm still labeled as one of the Big Apple's most eligible bachelors.

And my attraction to Ava only grew stronger because no other woman can compare.

Ava pulls the jacket closed in front and snuggles deeper into it like it's the most comfortable thing she's ever worn. My jacket looks good on her. I bet the tailored dress shirt I'm wearing would look even better. I picture her in nothing but my shirt. She's riding me like a Harley, her full tits bouncing with each thrust.

Shit. I run a hand through my black, wavy hair. "I meant what I said in the kitchen. I've got to stay focused on the expansion. We've got a lot riding on it."

And shit again. When I say the word *riding*, my dick strains against my pants, begging to get out and take Ava for the ride of her life.

I try to regroup. Refocus. Re-fucking-anything to keep my mind from going to fantasyland with Leo's sister. "I'll be spending a lot of time overseas. Maybe for the next couple of years." I shrug. "I just don't know how long it will take. The wheels turn much slower overseas than they do here. This is my responsibility and my idea, so I can't drop the ball." The financial risk is also much bigger than our market analysts anticipated. I don't want to let my partners down, so I'm going to work twenty-four-seven while I'm overseas to make sure this venture works. And so I don't turn out to be the loser my parents expected me to be once I joined forces with Leo. "Looks like I'll pretty much be living abroad until this project is finished and stable."

It's probably my imagination, but Ava seems to stop breathing. Finally, she asks, "When do you expect to leave?"

"A couple of weeks from now. Three at most. I'll come up with a plan with Oz and Leo, and hand off as many of my stateside responsibilities as I can. Then I'm gone."

"I'll miss you." I swear her voice is a soft, sad whisper.

I shake it off. "I'll miss you too, Rookie." I can't help the gloom in my own voice. I'll miss her so fucking much that my chest already aches, and I'm not even gone yet.

"Well…" She shifts and closes the small space between us. "…if you're leaving me…"

Like I said, her presence is like a blanket that wraps around me and pulls me in until my skin burns hot for her touch. I want to bury my face in her hair, then kiss her until she's too breathless to say anything but my name. I so could because we're standing in the shadowed corner of the balcony where the guests inside can't see us.

"And since you're my best friend and it's my birthday and all, I need a favor." Honest to God, there's a purr in her voice. "Think of it as a special birthday present."

"'Course," I say. "You know you can count on me." Truth is, I'd do anything for her. All she has to do is ask.

She stays silent for a beat, then she draws in a breath that's heavy. Almost wistful. "I've always been able to count on you as much as I can count on Leo." Her voice is low. "I'm sort of the sister you never had, right?"

I guess that's true, seeing as how I'm an only child. Except I don't look at Ava the way I'd expect to look at a sister. In fact, I'm positive I don't see her through the same lens as her brother.

"What's the favor, Rookie?"

"Promise you'll say yes?"

"Anything. Just name it." I pick up the glass and pull in a mouthful of whiskey. It singes my throat as it glides down to warm my insides.

She pulls that lip between her teeth and nibbles again. I can't fucking help myself. I almost come unglued right here and now. I'll get down on my hands and knees and crawl across broken glass if that's what she wants. And that glass I'd be crawling through? Even better if it shattered during the multiple ear-splitting orgasms I'd have just given her.

"You're a great lay, right?"

I sputter single malt scotch over the balcony, choking and coughing and gasping for air. I set my glass down on the railing again before I drop it.

"Jesus, Ava," I say when I can finally speak again. I should be used to her boldness and the way she constantly catches me off guard. No, that's an understatement. The way she constantly barrels through my guard, storms the gates, and takes no prisoners is a more accurate description.

"I need a date next weekend, and it needs to be someone impressive." Her tone takes a teasing turn down Naughty Lane. "And if you weren't a great lay with the looks and image to go with it, you wouldn't make it into the gossip magazines, right? I mean, look at you, Dex." Her hand sweeps my length. "With your black-as-sin hair, dark brooding eyes, olive complexion, and playboy smile, you obviously don't have any trouble getting laid. Women love you. Your whole *look* screams 'I'm great in bed.'"

Fuck's sake.

I take my Armani glasses off and pinch the corners of my eyes. "I haven't had any complaints in that department."

"I bet you haven't." The words roll off her tongue like velvet. "Which is why you're perfect. Everyone at my high school homecoming reunion will think I'm sleeping with a stud, but there won't be a big public breakup with tears or tantrums..." She taps her chin, and she's back in classic Ava mode. "Or one of us getting a sex change, which the gossip rags would probably love, but anyway..." She hauls in a breath. "So you'll do it?"

She looks up at me with big, blue eyes. They're begging me to say yes. I shouldn't. I really fucking shouldn't. A guy only has so much self-control, and this could ruin so many things. My business, my friendship with Leo. My friendship with Ava.

I fully intend to tell her I can't. It's a bad idea.

Imagine my surprise when I open my mouth and out pops, "Sure, I'll be your date."

Chapter Three

How can a smart guy be such a dumbass? Agreeing to be Ava's date isn't the most intelligent thing I've ever done. Not when I already want her so much, and she's completely off limits.

"Thanks, Dex." Ava throws her arms around my neck and kisses my cheek.

I scan the wall of glass to make sure none of the guests inside have discovered us lurking in the shadows of Leo's massive balcony. Swear to God, he could host the state fair on this patio.

She lingers against me, and my hands instinctively slide inside my jacket that is draped around her shoulders. My palms encase her hips so perfectly it seems like she's made for me. My fingers flex into her flesh to hold her in place for a few seconds more. I don't want to let her go.

In fact, I'd love to leave a bite mark on top of one of the hip bones pressing into my palms. Okay, I'd like to leave marks on both hip bones and a few spots in-between.

Her fingers curl into my shoulders, and she steps into me, touching her cheek to mine. Pressing her full, lush tits to my chest.

Lust riots through me, and my grip on her hips tightens.

She brushes her nose against my shoulder and pulls in a deep breath. "You're wearing Body Heat. One of my favorites." Ava knows the Checkmate products better than Leo, Oz, or me.

"Give the girl an A." I pull back and nod to my jacket where a square outline is barely visible. "There's something in the inside pocket for you."

She searches and withdraws the velvet jewelry box. "What's this?"

"Your birthday present, Rookie. Did you think I'd show up empty-handed?"

"You weren't empty-handed. You brought flowers." She smooths her fingers across the soft fabric.

"Go on. Open it."

The lid creaks as she eases it up. A sweet gasp slips through her lips when she sees the stack of bangle bracelets. The distant city lights glint off the handcrafted gold.

"They're gorgeous, Dex. You shouldn't have."

That's what I love about Ava. She's bossy and bold, but she's so down to earth and unassuming at the same time. She obviously had no expectations that her guests would show up bearing expensive gifts.

I take the bracelets out and toss the box onto the table. Then I slide them onto her wrist.

"I don't know what to say." She fingers them.

Ava Foxx doesn't know what to say. Huh.

I realize my hands somehow found their way back inside the jacket and are resting on her hips again.

She kisses my cheek. "Thank you."

"You're welcome, Rookie." My chest swells because of how much she obviously likes the gift.

She pulls her lip between her teeth like she's contemplating something.

"What is it?" Maybe I'm wrong. Maybe she doesn't like the bracelets. Maybe she hates bracelets. "You don't like them." It's not a question because I'm sure I've screwed up.

She laughs. "I love them." She pretends to rap her knuckles against the side of my head. It's her way of telling Oz, Leo, and me that we're being dense.

"Then what?"

She steps into me again and presses her cheek to mine. "Since you're going to be my date Saturday night, maybe we should get more comfortable with each other," she whispers against my ear.

"We're already comfortable with each other." There's no one I'm more comfortable with than Ava, except Oz and Leo. Ava and I are together a lot. We meet every morning for coffee before work, a habit we formed a few years ago when Ava was building our website. Checkmate was her first big client, and since I oversee our retail studios, I volunteered to work closely with her to ensure it conveyed our message and branding.

We grew so close during that time that we never gave up the morning ritual. It's not something we advertise. We don't want anyone to get the wrong idea, especially Ava's overprotective brother, who would likely *try* to kick my ass if he thought I was making moves on his sister. So we meet at a coffee shop pretty close to Checkmate headquarters but far enough away that we won't bump into my employees or my business partners.

It's dark on the balcony, but her huffy exhale tells me she's just rolled her eyes. I smile because I love that sassiness.

She pulls back to look at me, and moonlight glistens against her big, blue eyes. "We're comfortable with each other as friends, not like a couple who are dating." Her long, slender fingers are still curled into my shoulders. They're strong from a profession that requires endless hours working on a computer. Those skillful fingers apply just enough pressure to tell me she's not planning to let go.

And I'm so fucking glad.

So I slide one hand around to the small of her back and mold my palm against her. A current seeps through her dress and skates up my arm.

I swear, she draws in a sharp breath and holds it.

When I don't respond she asks, "Do you feel as comfortable with me as you do a woman you're sleeping with?" Her soft words are mingled with the scent of scotch, and they whisper over my cheeks.

Long, loose curls hang around her shoulders, and I want to brush them back and taste her neck. Feather soft, slow kisses along her jaw until I reach her ear where I'd breathe hot, filthy promises. She'd shiver, I'm sure of it. Maybe she'd tilt her head to one side to give me better access, which would tell me she wanted more dirty talk. Dirty talk is my specialty. And I'd give her all she wanted until she shattered without even getting her naked.

"Well, Dex?" Her words are low and timid, like she's afraid I won't give her the answer she's hoping for. "Do you?"

"'Course." Not exactly. I haven't felt anywhere near as comfortable with the women I've dated as I feel with Ava. Which is why I haven't dated much lately, no matter what the gossip rags say.

Some of the tension in her body eases, and she leans into me. "Then we should get more familiar with each other…" She swallows and looks toward Central Park. "You know…" She turns her attention to a button on my shirt. "We should look like a real couple."

I guess I *am* obtuse. Obviously, she's trying to tell me something, but I'm not catching on.

Her sigh is as big as Central Park.

"Why don't we make this easier on both of us?" I lace my fingers at the small of her back and pull her closer. "Tell me exactly what it is you're trying to say." I can't hide the smile in my voice. Ava doesn't beat around the bush. She usually takes a stick and whacks the fucking bush until there's no leaves left on it. So I find her sudden shyness not only amusing, but sexy as hell.

"Well, this is a good start. You're holding me like we're a couple." Nerves tremor through her last few words. "I want us to look real next weekend, so, um…" She gives me a one-shoulder shrug and fingers the button on my shirt that has suddenly become so fascinating. "Maybe we should kiss."

I go rigid and drop my hands to my sides. The moment I lose that intimate contact, my fingers tingle to touch her again.

"That's not a good idea, Ava." All amusement is gone from

my tone. We'd be treading on dangerous ground. Mostly because I already know how much I'd like it and wouldn't want to stop.

"*Come on*, Dex." She doesn't step back, and we're still so close, I could do exactly what she's asking and take her mouth with mine.

"Why don't you want to bring a real date, Ava?" I scrub a hand down my face. "There's what—eight million people in New York? Close to half of them have to be men." My geekster status roars back to life as I start doing the stats in my head. "Out of those, a large segment are single and—"

She puts a cupped hand over my mouth. "If you don't want to be my date, just say so. But you know as well as I do that Leo scares off every guy I meet. On the rare occasions that I've dated a guy more than once or twice, I kept it a secret."

Jealousy burns through me like wildfire at the thought of her with another man. I have no right to feel that way, though.

"If pictures of this reunion show up on social media, and I'm with a guy Leo has never met, he'll hunt him down, give him the third degree, have him followed, and probably try to pay the NSA to listen in on our phone calls."

True. Leo means well, but there's such a thing as overkill. He excels at it, especially when it comes to his sister.

But still...

My fingers encircle her slender wrist, and I pull her hand away from my mouth. She lets her palm fall to my chest, and my hand covers hers. "What about Leo? I'm sure he'd be glad to go with you." I'm kind of desperate now because all I can think of is how much I really do want to kiss this girl I've wanted for so long.

"Really? You want me to take my brother as my date?" My jacket tents at her side where she's put a hand on her hip.

She's got a point. A good one, actually, but goddamn. I need to find a way out of this. Leo will kill me if he catches me kissing his hot-as-hell sister.

"Leo's got commitments next weekend and can't go. Thank God, by the way, because he still treats me like a kid. I mentioned taking you, and he thinks it's a good idea," she says, squelching any hope I had of using the Leo-will-go-psycho card.

"Dex, please." Her voice goes silky soft.

She's begging me, and the sound pulls on the strings of my heart. It also makes my cock ache with need because of the fantasies it inspires.

Before I can respond, she says, "Please, please, *please*. Take me."

My throat closes. Swear to God, I think my vision even blurs. I adjust my glasses to make sure I've still got them on.

Oh, I want to take you, Rookie. Right here. Right now. Up against the wall. Or on the patio table. I'm good with it either way.

I try to focus on what she really means. "Of course I'll take you." I try not to choke when I say it, because my dirty mind is spiraling in every direction. Imagining her beneath me. Her bare, firm legs wrapped around my waist as I hover over her, teasing her pussy with my rock-hard prick. She's dripping wet and begging me to fuck her. I clear my throat and add, "To the reunion."

How hard can it be? No, I'm not talking about my cock. I already know it's as hard as fucking granite. I mean, a reunion lasts a few hours tops. Since Leo moved Ava to the city to live with him after their parents died, she graduated from a private high school in Gramercy Park. They'd probably have the reunion in their gym. I could pick her up, we'd have a few drinks, I'd put my arm around her to play my part. Then home alone with only my hand and a peek at Tumblr to finish off the night.

"Yay!" She bounces on her heels, and my eyes are drawn to that remarkable cleavage.

There's nothing I'd like more than to see those tits bounce as she rides me to one, two, ten orgasms. I'd sit up as she came and suck each one until the nipples were so hard they matched my dick. She'd cry out because they'd ache with pleasure from my tongue. Then I'd bury my face in them, and eventually, fuck them before the night was over.

"What time should I pick you up?"

"Oh, I forgot to mention." She bites her lip and looks away to scan the skyline.

Uneasiness settles in the pit of my stomach. Like I said, Ava doesn't tiptoe around anything. She uses steel-toed boots to stomp right over it.

"Ava."

She blows out an irritated breath. "The homecoming reunion is at my old high school upstate. They've asked several successful alumni to attend. I've done well in my career, especially for my age, so I'm on their list. But my personal life is a failure because of my numbskull brother bird-dogging me twenty-four-seven. I'm tired of it, Dex, but I can't very well fix the problem by this weekend."

Another good point. Yet the point that's captured my full attention right now is straining against my fly and throbbing like a motherfucker.

"All right, we can drive up early Saturday and drive back late Saturday night." There. Problem solved.

"Well..." Ava scans the inky sky again.

Shit. This isn't going to end well, I can already tell.

"The festivities are all weekend. We'll have to spend the weekend upstate."

I forget to breathe for a second. I might be thickheaded sometimes, but even I know what this means. I'm going to be alone with Ava all weekend. With no supervision from our inner circle. No one to hold us accountable. And no one to remind me why I shouldn't fuck the only woman I've wanted for the better part of two years.

Chapter Four

Hold the fucking phone. My brain is still spinning like the colorful wheel does on my computer when a program refuses to load. Not even the chilled autumn air clears my head as I try to process Ava's revelation that we'll be spending an entire weekend alone together upstate.

She leans into me and says, "Kiss me, Dex."

As we stand out on the shadowy balcony, away from the prying eyes of her birthday guests, I scramble for a way out of this impossible situation. I can't jeopardize my professional relationship with Leo. If the expansion derails, it could be the end of Checkmate. Plus, we've just weathered a public relations shit-storm, and things are running smoothly again. Why would I want to rock that boat when the ocean we're sailing on is smooth as fucking glass right now?

My gaze feathers over her silky skin, her pleading eyes, her full lips that are parted and ready for me to slip my tongue through and get my very first taste of heaven.

I can't say no to her. Hell no, I just can't. But I have to at least try to talk sense into her so maybe she'll change her mind.

"No time like the present to have a heart to heart with your brother so you can find a real date without sneaking around. You're a grown woman, Ava, and—"

Her palm molds over my mouth again, effectively shutting me the hell up. Goddammit. She's definitely the only person that can get away with *that*.

"You're damn right I'm a grown woman, Dex, and it's about time you noticed."

Oh, I've noticed. I'm not blind. Or gay. Or a dumbass.

Okay, fine. I'm not *always* a dumbass.

"You've always seen me as a little girl." Her voice is raspy and low. Her lips are pouty. It's so unlike Ava to sulk, but it's the sexiest damn thing I've seen in months. "Like a kid sister, and I want that to stop."

If she'd say this to her thick-headed brother, we wouldn't be in this mess. I could kiss her any damn time I wanted.

"I want you to take me seriously." She hesitates. "And I want you to kiss me like you mean it." Another pause, her hand still clamped over my mouth.

We stand as still as statues. Gazes locked. Breaths heavy. Bodies hot.

The air around us thickens and vibrates with a hum of energy. Desire pulses through me until I can't think of anything else except fulfilling her request. The lady wants to be kissed. Good friend and nice guy that I am, it's practically a civic duty to give her what she wants.

My lips part, and I pull the tip of her finger in. I let my tongue flick over it, then I suck.

She inhales a sharp breath and holds it.

I mold my palm over the back of her hand and take turns sucking and licking each of her fingers without breaking eye contact. When I've given each finger its due, I bite and tongue my way to the inside of her wrist, where I feather soft kisses.

A sexy sound escapes her, but she doesn't speak. Which tells me how much she likes what I'm doing to her because Ava is rarely speechless.

"Be careful what you ask for, Rookie." My voice has gone husky, and my hot breath against her tender flesh causes a shudder to race over her. I let my lips curl up as I press an openmouthed kiss to that same spot and hold her gaze with mine.

The dark, smoky look in her eyes tells me she's mesmerized. She's still bundled into my jacket, so I reach up and curl my fingers around the lapel. Gently, I tug her until she's flush against me. I take my time. Draw out the moment. And never let my stare release hers.

I smooth the back of one finger across her cheek, down her neck, and stop just short of that magnificent cleavage. Her heart pounds against my touch.

The bold, brazen Ava I know is gone, replaced with a side of her I've never seen. Her expression is open and honest, like she's baring her soul to me, opening her heart to me like she's never done for anyone else. It makes me want her all the more, and not just the kiss that I'm sure is about to rock our world. I want all of her.

I can't hold back another second. My head dips forward, and she follows my lead, tilting her head back. It happens at the exact same moment, like she's so in tune to me that she can anticipate my every move.

Her lips part as my mouth covers hers. A hungry, wanting moan comes from her and drives me on. I angle her head to deepen the kiss, slide my hand around her neck, up her nape, and thread my fingers through her hair. It's silky soft and slides over my skin.

Her tongue flicks across mine, and a shock of lust rushes through me.

I lace a hand inside the jacket and anchor it around her waist, pulling her tighter. She molds and melts into me to perfection. She slides her hands up my chest and circles her arms around my neck. This time, I moan and slip a thigh between her legs.

She tastes like fresh morning dew, and I can't help but think she's exactly the kind of girl I want to stay curled up with in bed on a cold rainy day. I'd get to know every inch of her body, and when we were done, we'd listen to the thunder and rain pelting the windows as we drifted off to sleep.

A hint of Macallan lingers on her mouth, and I trace her lips with the tip of my tongue.

"You're such a good kisser," she whispers with her eyes closed.

I nip at the corner of her mouth. "So are you, Rookie." If she weren't one of my closest friends and my business partner's sister, I'd show her how good I am at so much more. I'd have her up against the wall, her dress hiked up to her waist, and my dick pounding so deep into her that we'd get arrested for disturbing the peace. When I was finished with her, she'd be satisfied, satiated, and so thoroughly fucked she wouldn't need a man for another year.

I might sound pretty full of myself, but I wouldn't have it any other way if I were lucky enough to find myself in that position with Ava. Or any other position she wanted to try.

Not gonna happen, though.

Too bad because I could go all night with the hard-on I've got right now. I could probably go all weekend with this boner. My dick swells at the thought of having an entire weekend in bed with Ava.

"No, I'm not," she whispers as I brush my lips across hers.

"Not what?" I ask with another graze of our mouths because I'm not following her meaning.

"Not a good kisser. Or a good lover." She opens her mouth, and I taste her again.

"Why would you say that?" I murmur against her lips.

Her sigh is heavy. Eyes still closed. "Because I've never had an orgasm."

I freeze. I pull away just enough so our noses graze. "*Huh?*" I ask. There's that high intelligence factor rearing its head again.

"At least not with anyone else in the room." Ava rests her forehead against my chin. "I wasn't kidding about not dating much. I swear, I asked for a frequent flyer card from the adult toyshop down the street from my apartment. It's the only way I can get laid."

So many things are spiraling through my mind right now: a) She's never had an orgasm without battery-operated assistance? Holy shit. b) She's obviously been dating the wrong guys. And

c) Back to the battery-operated assistance. I can't get the image out of my mind. Ava getting herself off with a vibrator, her other hand flying over her clit. Maybe she's looking at Tumblr or porn while she does it.

Or thinking of me kissing her, eating her, fucking her.

I grind my teeth into dust to keep from coming like a kid having a wet dream.

If Leo weren't one of my best friends and my business partner, I'd tell him to fuck-off, toss Ava over one shoulder, and run to my apartment just around the corner. She'd know what she's been missing within minutes, guaranteed.

Another revelation barrels right over me. She really is a rookie. In more ways than one. And I want to be the one to teach her until she's a damn expert on the subject of orgasms. The thought of another guy delivering her very first man-made orgasm makes my jaw go on lock down.

I bite my tongue to keep from blurting the thing that's racing through my mind, because "bend over and I'll fix your problem" probably isn't the best comeback. She needs to be consoled. Encouraged.

Okay, let's be honest. She *does* need to be bent over and shown the ropes by a master. There *is* no better solution to her problem than that.

But I can't. So back to what I should say to offer comfort as a friend.

"See?" she finally says to break the earsplitting silence. "You can't even respond. Do you understand why I need you to be my date? I might be good at my profession, but when it comes to men, I suck."

Dear God. I am *not* picturing her sucking right now. No way am I thinking about her lips wrapped around my dick, her cheeks sunken in from the suction, her head bobbing up and down while I run my fingers through her hair.

"And do you see why I need you to kiss me now, so it looks

real at the reunion?"

I swallow down the cotton in my mouth. I can do this. She needs me. What are friends for?

I place the edge of my index finger under her chin and lift her gaze to mine. "One day it will happen, but in the meantime..." I brush my lips across hers and drop my voice to a throaty whisper. "You're so *fucking* beautiful that any man is lucky to be with you." I stress the F-bomb since she thinks it's sexy. "You should take your *fucking* time before giving any man the privilege of dating you," I whisper against her lips. "You're so goddamn special that you should be very selective who you *fuck*."

The last F-bomb pushes her over the edge, and she devours my mouth with hers in a ravenous kiss.

Her hands are flat against my chest, and her long, slender fingers flex into my pecs. The muscle I've packed on at the gym over the years, thanks to friendly fitness competitions with Leo and Oz, jump under her touch.

We're swept away by the wanting, the intimacy of the kiss. I'm just as lost in it as she is, and I can't help but wonder if she's as wet as I am hard. I'd love to sink my fingers into her pussy and find out for myself.

A deep pain of regret stabs me in the chest. No way can I go away with her now. Not after this. It would take a miracle for me not to fuck her in every possible position so she knows what she's been missing.

"There you are." Leo's voice comes from behind me. "We've been looking for you two. Chloe's ready to light the candles on your birthday cake, Ava."

My back is to the door, and I'm so much bigger than Ava that I'm shielding her from view. She takes a step back, and reality crashes over me like a bucket of ice water. I was so lost in the fantasy of finally kissing the girl I've wanted for so long, I didn't hear the door slide open.

She steps around me. "Hey, numbskull," she says to her

brother in that playful sibling tone they use with each other. I've always been oddly envious of their closeness since I'm an only child. "I was just talking to Dex about the reunion."

Ava goes to join Leo at the door, and I follow, grabbing my drink from the railing on the way.

"Dude," Leo says to me. "You're doing me a solid by going with her."

He slaps me on the back as I walk past him and step into the apartment. The chatter of the guests escalates as the lights dim and Chloe emerges from the kitchen with a gorgeous custom cake shaped like a computer. It's covered in burning candles and glows in the dark room. Leo falls in beside me, and I stop on the fringe of the crowd to watch Ava join Chloe at the table. Everyone starts to sing *Happy Birthday To You*.

"I wouldn't trust anyone else to watch out for her, you know?" Leo leans over and speaks to me through the din of alcohol-laced party voices that are cheerfully off tune. "Thanks, man. I owe you one."

I don't want Leo to see my jaw turn to stone, so I hide it behind a drink of Macallan and shove my other hand in my pocket. I swallow down the smooth, stout liquid. I should man up and tell him I can't go, but I guess Ava and I both have a problem being up front with her brother.

"Sure. Any time," I say.

I doubt Leo would think he owes me anything except maybe an ass kicking if he knew the truth. He's sending his sister off for a weekend with exactly the kind of man he's been trying to protect her from since she was sixteen.

That's right. Me. Dex Moore. Shitty business partner. Even shittier friend. I want to talk dirty to Ava Foxx while I deliver an earth-moving orgasm. Her first. And the best she'll ever have.

Chapter Five

"Sorry I'm late, but I lost my panties on the way over here," Ava says as she marches up to our usual table in the back corner of the Bump & Grind. She gives me a perturbed look and slides into the chair across from me.

I've already fixed her coffee the way she likes it, but I stop stirring my Black Eye.

I spent the weekend coming up with a plan for her reunion so I won't cross a line I shouldn't. I even got here a few minutes earlier than our usual seven-thirty AM meet-up time so I could think through what I'm going to say. But now my mind blanks. Did she just say she isn't wearing panties?

"Um," I finally manage to say. Yeah, yeah, I know. My vocabulary is astounding.

"I mean, *who* loses their panties on the subway during Monday morning rush hour?"

I got nothin'.

Swear to God, I catch myself leaning forward to look over the table. That deep purple sweater dress she's wearing is so damn clingy that one good look is all I need to determine the status of her lingerie. Or lack of...

She huffs again, and I lean back in my chair. She adjusts the stylish scarf around her neck, slings her purse—which is the size of an RV—off one shoulder and plops it in another chair. The city is alive and flowing with energy as the foot traffic bustles past the glass window behind her.

The scent of her soap and shampoo drifts to me like she's just stepped out of the shower. I'm warmed from the inside out as I breathe in that comforting smell of rain clouds. Fresh. Feminine. Familiar.

She leans into me and draws in a deep breath. It's part of our morning ritual. She tries to guess which Checkmate cologne I'm wearing, and it's always the favorite part of my whole damn day.

"Wicked Temptation." She never misses.

"Give the girl an A." As a reward, I push the coffee in front of her. She and Leo both have a *thing* about coffee. They like it mixed up with just the right amounts of cream, raw sugar, and vanilla. It has something to do with their parents, but neither one of them will talk about it.

"Thanks, Dex." Her tone softens, and she wraps her lips over the rim of the cup and sips. Her eyes slide shut, and she moans her approval.

I'm mesmerized by her soft moan, her full lips, the muscles in her slender neck that move as the bold brew slides down her throat. Add in my insatiable curiosity over panties or no-panties, and I've got a pretty good porn flick going on in my head.

"This is so good." She opens her eyes. "You do it exactly the way I like it."

I can't help it. I lick my lips. "My pleasure."

Her lips curl into a smile, and I know we're not talking about coffee anymore.

I clear my throat. "So how did your panties go rogue?" I have to ask.

She blows out a breath that causes the tendrils of silky hair framing her face to flutter and then settle back against her cheeks. "I brought fresh clothes to the gym this morning." She takes another drink. "But I dropped my purse getting on the train, and it spilled everywhere. I thought I found everything, but when I went to get dressed after my workout, my panties were missing."

My brilliant mind forms several deductions based on what she's just said. Some perv probably has her panties, I now know the reason for the suitcase-sized purse, and she's definitely commando under that dress. My fingers curve around my coffee cup. It's the only way I can stop myself from leaning over to check out her missing panty lines.

She leans forward in the most intimate way and whispers, "Your eyes just dilated. You're picturing me pantyless, aren't you?"

Hell yes. I shrug. "I'm a guy. 'Course I am."

She gives me a naughty smile. "Sorry to disappoint, but I'm fully clothed. I swung by my apartment and got a new pair. That's why I'm late."

Blood starts to flow to my brain again. Thank God, because it was all going to my dick when I thought she was bare under that hot-as-sin dress. But now I'm wondering one thing: what color are they? Okay, two things: is it a thong?

"I booked two rooms at the Hilton in your hometown," I blurt. Apparently, not all the blood has circulated back into my head. It has to be done, though. I made sure the rooms were on different floors. "And I got us two train tickets." Public transportation is part of my plan too. Basically, my strategy is to spend as little time alone with Ava as possible during our weekend away together.

She shakes her head and downs more coffee. "I've got our accommodations taken care of so cancel your reservations. The train is out of the question. Do you have any idea how much I pack to go on a trip?"

If the purse is any indication, she probably needs a moving truck to carry her luggage. But alone in a car with Ava all the way upstate and back will be torture for me. Especially if she smells as good as she does right now. I won't need to wear cologne. She's the very definition of *Wicked Temptation*.

"I don't want to lug all of that onto a train. Can you drive since I don't have a car?" Ava grabs her purse and starts rummaging through it. I swear, she could swan dive into that thing.

I'm just about to give her the long list of irrefutable reasons why taking the train is a much better idea when someone squeezes my shoulder.

"Hello, Dex," a silky voice purrs into my ear.

Ava stops rummaging, and her head pops up to stare over my shoulder.

Her fresh scent is replaced by a thick, rich perfume I'd expect to encounter at a posh country club in the Hamptons. Not a busy coffee shop on a Monday morning in Manhattan.

I glance over my shoulder and bite back a cuss word.

"Cynthia," I say. Actually, the name *Cynthia Ethridge* is a cuss word in my book. She's attractive, mid-thirties, and wearing a haute couture dress that matches her perfume.

And I don't feel a damn thing when I look at her. The only woman that kick-starts my pulse, makes my chest go tight, and sets the gears of my dirty mind in motion is Ava. The one girl I can't have.

Mrs. Ethridge slides into the empty seat to my left without an invitation.

"Sure. Have a seat." I don't even try to hide the smartass tone in my voice.

"You look great," she says.

I can't help but notice that her lips are a little fuller than the last time I saw her. So are her tits. Props to her plastic surgeon, but I prefer women with a more authentic look. I also prefer them single, and Cynthia's seventy-eight-year-old, filthy rich husband who doesn't mind if she strays once in a while was a deal-breaker.

"Thanks." I can't bring myself to return the compliment. Mostly because I'm looking at Ava, and her face has gone a little pale. A surge of anger courses through me. "Cynthia, I'm having a private conversation here, so—"

"Ava Foxx." Ava sticks a hand out. "Nice to meet you."

Cynthia shakes her hand and sizes Ava up like she's the competition. No fucking way. Cynthia's name might as well be Barbie, while Ava is all woman. And temptation. Wicked

Temptation.

I don't want to be rude, but I want Cynthia gone. I was straight up with her when I broke it off. "Look—"

"I'm Dex's friend," Ava blurts. She throws her purse over a shoulder, stands, and sweeps her coffee off the table. "More like a sister, really. Right, Dex?"

What the fuck? I give her a fierce look, trying to communicate "sit your pretty little ass down and have my back like I'm going to have yours this weekend."

Does absolutely no good.

"Three's a crowd." She won't look me in the eye. "I've got to get to work anyway." She fingers the bracelets I gave her for her birthday. She pretends to readjust them. "Okay, so see you later."

Then she's gone, leaving me with a woman I have zero interest in and who has just ruined my whole goddamn day.

I turn a cast iron stare on Cynthia. She's looking very pleased with herself, like she's won a round of *Take The Guy To My Secret Loft In The Village And Fuck Him*. Never gonna happen.

"Don't ever do that again," I say as I stand.

Her expression turns to shock, but I don't wait around to see if it morphs into anger because she's not getting the prize after all.

I tumble onto the sidewalk and look both ways for Ava. Good thing I'm tall. I can see over a lot of the crowd. A whiz of deep purple catches my eye. She's already halfway down the block and walking like she can't get away fast enough. Her head is down, like she's looking at her phone.

I push through the crowd and try to catch up.

"Ava," I shout.

She either doesn't hear me or she ignores me. Not sure which, but she crosses the intersection. I hurry to make the cross too, but the light flashes red, and I'm stuck.

I pull my phone from my pocket and shoot her a text.

Slow down, Rookie.

The dots jump.

I'm in a hurry. Talk later?

Damn straight, we'll talk.

The light is still red, and Ava is getting smaller in the distance. Then she glances over her shoulder, and my heart squeezes. She doesn't just look upset. She looks hurt. I can't figure this girl out. I mean, I know we have this special bond. One minute, I think it goes much, much deeper. The next, I'm reminded it doesn't. Like last night when she kissed me like a lover, then introduced herself as my friend and almost-sister a few minutes ago in the coffee shop.

But Ava hurt over Cynthia? I can't let it go. I fire off another text.

Let's talk now.

The fucking light finally allows me to cross, and I eat up the pavement with long strides. Ava looks back again, and I wave because I think she sees me. Guess not, because she veers to the curb, hails a cab, and jumps in.

I stop and stare at the back of the yellow cab as it drives away. My phone dings.

Can't. Sorry. Too much work waiting at the office.

All I can think is I've never hated taxis so much in my life.

Chapter Six

"Dex." Oz snaps his fingers in front of my face to break me out of the trance. He's perched on the edge of my desk. "What the hell has gotten into you?"

A petite blonde with the ass of an angel and a purse as big as her attitude.

"Are you still jet lagged?" Leo's seated on my office sofa and doesn't look up from the four thousand dollar hand-carved chessboard I picked up in Italy several years back.

I lean back in my executive chair, prop both feet on my desk, and take off my glasses to rub my eyes. This meeting is important. We need to discuss a solution to the foreseeable problems with the expansion. The least I can do is pay attention and stop thinking of Ava.

But hurting Ava is something I can't get out of my head, and it's driving me batshit crazy. I've texted her several more times, but gotten no response.

I release a breath so heavy that papers shift and flutter on my desk. "Not jet lagged. This new venture is already kicking my ass, and we're just getting started."

Leo's head pops up. "Should we pull back? Put the expansion on pause for a while?"

I shake my head and thrum my fingers against the leather arm of my chair. "That's not the answer. This is a good move for Checkmate." I clear my throat, trying to keep a confident tone so I don't alarm my partners. Fear is contagious, and now isn't the time to bail on this project. "Just more costly than we expected. Otherwise, we've done the research and market analysis, and laid the groundwork. It's time to move forward." I won't give up on this and become the failure my parents predicted I'd be when I teamed up with Leo and Oz instead of pursuing something "worthy of my intellect." I'll make this work and come through for my partners.

"This is your baby," Oz says. "Tell us how we can help make it happen."

This is the hard part. During my latest trip abroad, it became clear we needed someone on-site to manage the project. Since the expansion is my idea, that someone should be me. After kissing Ava at her birthday party, I've realized how much I don't want to leave her behind. Realized how much I'll miss her.

Two and two isn't adding up to four because we're just friends. Almost family. I can't hinge the future of this company on a relationship with a woman that will never go beyond friendship.

Leticia, Leo's assistant and right arm, marches past the glass forward-facing wall of my office and raps a knuckle against the open door. I wave her in and keep talking. She's efficient, smart as a whip, and keeps Checkmate running like a well-oiled machine using just an iPad and her pointing finger. Her husband assures us that she also runs their kids' soccer teams better than the pros. Anyone who can corral that many energetic kids has my vote of confidence. There's no one we trust more.

"We need to cut fat out of our company budget to offset the extra costs. I think we should hand the reins of the stateside studios to Magnus and Gerard," I say. "They can handle my responsibilities here just as well as I can. I'll rent a flat in both Dubai and Europe and travel back and forth to New York as needed."

"It's going to be weird without you here all the time," Leo says. "It's always been the three of us together. We don't make decisions without each other."

Oz coughs something that sounds like *"bullshit"* behind his hand. I wrinkle my forehead to say "really?" It wasn't long ago that Leo definitely made a huge decision without Oz and me.

Leo refuses to acknowledge our smartass comebacks. He makes a move on the board, snatches up one of Oz's chess pieces, and analyzes it.

Oz chuckles and goes to study the board.

In the face of a public relations nightmare, Leo took our female PR account rep to Checkmate's anchor studio on Fifth Avenue. Without telling Oz and me, Leo lifted the veil of mystery that protects our trade secrets.

Keeping the secrets behind that curtain of privacy was a pact the three of us made from the beginning. If our clients want to pretend they came out of the womb looking cool, that's up to them. None of our concern. So one of us breaking that sacred pact shook our foundation. Especially since we'd agreed never to let a woman come between us.

When we started the company and Leo insisted we look the part of successful businessmen, I knew we'd stumbled into a gold mine. Helping men transform their image, their whole approach to life, and their relationships was an underserved market niche.

That's where I got the bright idea for Checkmate's retail studio arm. We had our architect come up with a design that looked stylish yet masculine, called them Lifestyles Studios instead of stores, assigned each client a personal coach, offered client privacy so no one would know their newer, slicker images were purchased, and bingo. Men ate that shit up like candy. Still do.

Turns out, Leo, being the smart guy he is, trusted the right person with our secrets. She used them to stem the scandal and restore our image. Then Leo asked her to marry him. A regular fairy tale where the guy gets the girl, and the world is set right.

Oz finally takes Leo's rook and resumes his spot on the edge of my desk. "I've got dibs on his office," he says to Leo. "His view is better than mine."

"I get the chess sets and the desk," Leo deadpans.

I roll my eyes. Which makes me think of Ava again. She's the world's most dramatic, not to mention the world's sexiest eye-roller.

Leticia snatches the chess piece from Leo's hand and looks at me. "I'm not going to let them touch a thing in your office, Dex." She offers me a motherly smile. "It will be exactly the way you left it." She gives both Leo and Oz a pointed look. "And it will be waiting for you when you move back for good." She sets the piece next to the board and holds up her iPad. "In case you three geniuses haven't noticed, I'm pretty good with this thing. You can FaceTime every day if needed."

I chuckle. Truth is, it won't be the same without all three of us here. Together. Changing the status quo is never easy. It will likely put a strain on the company and on our partnership.

Leticia says to Leo, "If you boys are done, your fiancée is on line one."

Leo jumps up and all but sprints to his office.

Leticia winks at me, then leaves too.

"So what's really bothering you?" Oz asks.

"What?" Oh. Shit. "Nothing. Why would anything be bothering me?"

"Don't make me cough 'bullshit' behind my hand again."

"Fuck you."

Oz pushes off of my desk and heads for the door. "Fuck you too. You know where to find me if you need to talk," he says over one shoulder.

I'm alone again, thank fuck, so I snatch up my phone to see if Ava has returned any of my texts. She hasn't, and I want to crush the phone against the wall.

All of my dreams are about to come true. This expansion will make Checkmate the worldwide success I've dreamt it could be. We'll be even richer than we already are—thank you very much, Mom and Dad. I'll have proven that starting Checkmate Inc. instead of pursuing a career in the tech world wasn't a foolish mistake. I'm young, healthy, and have the whole fucking world at my feet. Life should be good.

So why do I feel like my happiness, my entire reason for living, is tethered to the silent phone in my hand?

Chapter Seven

The week has crawled by, mostly because I haven't seen Ava since she ran out of the coffee shop on Monday morning after Cynthia showed up and looked ready to dry hump me in public. Ava's texts sounded cheerful and upbeat, but when I explained that Cynthia was nothing to me, Ava responded with, *You'd owe me an explanation if we were sleeping together, which we're not because we're like family...*

Then she canceled our early morning coffee meets because of the amount of work she had to accomplish before our trip upstate.

The only time I go this long without seeing her is when one of us is out of town. I'm anxious to lay my eyes on her. Each day that's passed has made me more eager to spend time with her, even though spending the weekend alone probably isn't the best idea. Especially after the fantasies that have occupied my mind since our make-out session at her birthday party where she revealed she's never had a *real* orgasm.

When I turn onto Ava's street in the West Village, I'm lucky enough to find a parking spot just a few blocks away from her apartment. I ease my Porsche 911 into the empty space, climb out, and flick the remote.

There's a certain energy that flows through the city every Friday as New Yorkers prepare for the weekend. Today is no exception, and an electric current hums through me during the two-block walk. I tell myself it's the chilled autumn air, and I breathe it deep into my lungs, adjust the wool scarf around my neck, and stuff my cold hands into the lined pockets of my leather bomber jacket.

The air is cold enough to cause my breath to fog, and it swirls around me as I make my way up the steps of Ava's apartment building. I ring the bell, anticipation coursing through me.

"Dex?" Her voice streams through the intercom, and my pulse dials up a notch.

"It's me, Rookie."

She buzzes me in, and I take the stairs two at a time. The door to her apartment is open, and she's waiting. Of course I've been here before, but I never stayed long. Never wanted to deal with the temptation. Never wanted to *fall* to the temptation. Stepping inside is like jumping into an ocean of warmth. I'm totally immersed in her scent, her presence. Everything about the apartment is so Ava, and it feels so fucking good, like I've been without her for a year.

The space is small but neat and well organized. The decorations are eclectic and make a bold statement with colors and shapes and angles. The flowers I gave her for her birthday are displayed on the coffee table, far from fresh anymore. I close the door behind me and ease around to take her in. She's adorable in a pair of snug jeans, a deep plum cashmere sweater, and ankle boots. The bracelets I gave her glint at me. A knit beanie slouches to one side of her head, and her hair is pulled back in a ponytail with wisps hanging loose to brush against her cheeks and neck.

The hum of electricity that started when I pulled up out front speeds and starts to sing through my veins. "Hey," I manage to say. I'm so verbose I amaze myself sometimes. No surprise that I graduated Magna Cum Laude, right?

"Hey." Ava's glossy lips shimmer as she speaks.

I swear I can hear the clock on her wall ticking as we do nothing but stare at each other, and I hate it. Not looking at her. I could never hate that. Staring at Ava is my favorite pastime and probably the only thing I like more than playing chess or working at Checkmate. It's the awkward strain in our relationship that I hate. It's never been like that between us.

"Bedroom Eyes," she says.

Huh? Was I really looking at her that way? "What?" I shift my weight, afraid I'm totally busted.

"You're wearing Bedroom Eyes. It's one of Checkmate's newest colognes."

Oh. Right. "Give the girl an A." Finally, I unglue my feet from the floor and walk to her. I press a soft kiss to her cheek. "Be warned, I'm in a grumpy-ass mood. At least that's what Oz and Leo called it. I refused to admit it to them, but they may be right. I think it's because I haven't had a decent cup of coffee all week."

She slugs my arm. "I'll make it up to you and buy you a cup on our way out of town."

I flinch and pretend she really packs a punch by rubbing my arm. "Now you owe me two cups."

"I'll get my things." She disappears into her bedroom and emerges with enough luggage to clothe a third world country. Swear to God, getting all of that onto the train would've been easier than it's going to be fitting it into my Porsche.

Her purple suitcase could shelter a small elephant. Attached to the handle by a long strap is a matching monogramed bag. It's smaller, but that's not saying much.

"The small one is my cosmetics bag," she says.

I'm unable to stop my jaw from hanging open.

"What?" She holds out her hand, palm up. "That's how I roll." She swings her gigantic purse over a shoulder, grabs the suitcase handle, and tries to sashay to the door. The key word here is *tries*. A fight between Ava and the suitcase breaks out, and it's obvious she's about to go down in defeat.

It's my turn to roll my eyes, and I grab the bags. "Allow me."

"Thank you." She bats those big, blue eyes at me, and I'm toast.

I do not eye-fuck her ass all the way down the stairs. I am not mesmerized by the sway of her hips and the way those distressed jeans mold to her toned thighs as we make our way down the street. And my mind absolutely does not go in nine different dirty directions when she drops her sunglasses on the sidewalk next to my car and bends over to pick them up.

Nuh-uh, not me. I'm the master of control and keep my mind out of the gutter by thinking of chess. Only I want to play strip chess with Ava, and that's where my mind wanders.

Fuck.

I manage to pack her mammoth luggage into the trunk. "*Ouch.*" I moan and rub my lower back. I limp to the passenger door and open it, waving her in.

"Oh my God! The suitcase threw your back out?"

I try not to laugh, but her owlish eyes are too cute for her own good. Too innocent. A wave of worry washes over me at how some guys might try to take advantage of that, and I understand why Leo hasn't been able to let go of the overprotective big brother routine.

Her lips round into an "O" to match her eyes, and I can't hold onto the fake grimace any longer. My involuntary smile has her wide eyes narrowing. I break into all out laughter, and she slugs my arm again.

She slides into the passenger seat, and I lean in. "I'll visit my chiropractor next week and send you the bill." I close the door before she can deliver another playful punch.

Before you know it, the sporty German engine is roaring through the Lincoln Tunnel. We make a quick stop in New Rochelle for a cup of joe, and we're off again. The drive upstate is gorgeous. Splashes of vibrant red, orange, yellow, and purple whiz past. I should feel like I've got everything I need or want in life.

But something's different. Something's missing.

I can't remember Ava ever being this distant.

It's reminiscent of my childhood. Stiff. Uncomfortable. Detached. My parents were distant and distracted by academic pursuit, only offering a glimmer of emotion when I brought home the latest "A" on a test or another first place ribbon from a science fair or math competition. Nothing like the unconditional acceptance I get from Ava. Until now.

"So," her fingers slide over the gold bracelets as she speaks, "how are the plans to move overseas coming along?"

Coldness seeps into my chest right over my heart. Her question reminds me that my life is about to change drastically, and she won't be as much a part of it. That seems unfathomable. I don't see our relationship going beyond friendship, though. Not without starting a war with Leo. Even if he came around in the end, I know beyond a shadow of a doubt that he'd overreact in the beginning, and it could do irreparable damage to his bond with Ava.

I know what it's like to be lonely. To be alone without family to lean on. I won't risk that happening to two of the people I care most about in the world. I couldn't live with myself if I were the cause of such disappointment and heartbreak, because I'm so familiar with how deeply it cuts.

I can't bring myself to describe my plans to move as *good*. "The plans are coming along. Leticia is trying to line up flat rentals. If we don't find something quickly enough, I can live in a hotel."

"Sounds like quite a life, living in Europe and Dubai. Hopping from one exotic location to the next. You'll be earning that rep in the gossip rags."

"I'll be working around the clock, and it's a temporary arrangement." Two fucking years away from New York City, away from my office at Checkmate HQ...away from Ava doesn't seem all that temporary. It seems like a goddamn eternity, especially since she could very well meet someone and tie the knot in that amount of time.

My hands tighten around the steering wheel, and I grow quiet as I try to focus on the road instead of the surge of jealousy burning through my veins.

"Well, it sounds like a blast. I'm sure it'll be the experience of a lifetime," Ava says.

It would be if she went with me. Or if I knew she'd be waiting for me when I got back. Neither is a possibility, though, and even if it were, I'd never ask it of her.

Chapter Eight

My Porsche is more than a little conspicuous when we pull into the small town where Ava and her brother grew up. Weatherton is charming and quaint with a stone church on the main drag and a few people meandering down the sidewalk in no particular hurry.

"Which hotel?" I ask, so we can unload, unpack, and get cleaned up for tonight. During the drive up, Ava informed me that tonight's alumni party kicks off the homecoming reunion.

"Turn left at the next light." She points up ahead.

I'm a little confused. When I Googled hotels as part of my *Don't Fuck Ava* plan, all four were located along this main road that runs from one end of town to the other. That's equivalent to about a six-minute car ride, so I know Ava can't be lost. Maybe there's a Bed and Breakfast in the area.

I turn left, and the road twists and turns through a residential neighborhood of small homes that look as though they should have apple pies cooling in the windows. A street hockey game is in progress, and the kids scatter to let us through, gawking and pointing at my sports car. We wave and ease down the lane.

"Turn right here." Ava points.

"I have no idea where we're going. I should've let you drive." I flip my blinker on and turn right onto another residential street that takes us deeper into the neighborhood.

She shakes her head. "Can't. I don't know how."

My foot comes down hard on the brake. We're sitting idle in the middle of the road, but I don't care. It's not like I'm holding up a line of traffic in this little town. "You don't know how to drive?"

"Nope," she says, and shrugs. "My parents died right before they were going to teach me." She looks away when she mentions her parents. "Then I moved to the city to live with Leo, and there was no need."

How do I not know this? "You really are a rookie," I tease her. My gaze drops to her shimmering, glossy lips. "In so many ways."

Her lips part, and a charge of electricity stirs the air between us. We both know I'm not talking about driving, but it's just wishful thinking on my part.

"Maybe you can help me out with that." Her voice is a feathery whisper, filled with promise, hunger, and need.

My dick grows so hard I almost moan. I want nothing more than to help her both behind the wheel and between the sheets. But I can't. "Ava—"

"This is a perfect neighborhood for driving lessons, don't you think?" She waves a hand across the span of the windshield.

Maybe I was projecting. Must be the double shot of espresso I ordered in my coffee, because nowhere in that sentence did she mention wanting help with her first man-made orgasm.

"While we're here, you could teach me...so many things," Ava adds with a sexy purr in her voice.

Good to know I wasn't projecting.

Before I can respond, she says, "My old house is just down the street on the left."

I'm so surprised that it takes me longer than it should to return my attention to the road and lift my foot from the brake. "We're going to the house where you and Leo grew up?" I know Leo hasn't been back to the house since his parents died, but he and Ava still own it. I also know they don't stay here when they make their annual autumn trek upstate to visit their parents' graves. I slowly accelerate down the block and glance at the clock on my dash. We've got plenty of time before checking into whatever hotel Ava has booked for us, so it won't hurt to take this trip down memory lane.

"Here it is."

I turn into the drive of a one-story home with white siding, a wraparound porch, and a screen door. The driveway leads down the side of the house, where I park in front of a one-car garage. The hedges are unusually manicured for a home that's been vacant for eight years.

"Can you keep a secret?" The corner of her mouth lifts. She lowers her sunglasses and peeks over the rim. Those vivid blue eyes are dimmed with sadness.

"For you? 'Course."

I kill the engine, but I don't get out. I look at Ava, wanting to hear her secret. Wanting to gauge her reaction to the familiar setting and the happy childhood I know she and Leo had, which was ripped away so suddenly and so tragically.

"I pay a landscaper and a cleaning service to keep the place looking nice. I also take the train alone once in a while and stay here overnight. It makes me feel like I'm surrounded by my parents." She pushes the swanky Ray-Bans up her perfectly shaped nose so her eyes are hidden, but a tremor threads through her words.

It occurs to me that Ava and I were both abandoned by our parents at a young age, just in different ways. My parents are still alive, but I long to experience the comfort of a close, loving family—something mine never was. Ava's family had been a Norman Rockwell painting, but they were taken from her far too soon. I'm not sure which is worse.

"Don't tell Leo, okay? He'd probably want to start coming with me out of his crazy sense of protectiveness. It's too painful for him to come back here. I don't want to put him through that."

I don't like lying to Leo, but I don't have to mention it either. This is something Ava needs, so I'll keep her secret. "No one has to know but you and me, Rookie."

"Thanks, Dex." She quickly climbs out of the car, and I swear I hear her sniff.

The inside surprises me. The furniture and décor are new. She's obviously had some remodeling done because there's a fresh coat of paint on the walls and new hardwood floors.

The house is cold, so Ava turns on the heat. I browse the den where family pictures still line the mantle. Very few of the shots are posed. Most of the pictures are of special impromptu moments: Leo holding a blue ribbon at a chess tournament, Ava learning to ride a bike, all four members of the Foxx clan opening Christmas presents, their parents kissing under a sprig of mistletoe.

I can't remember my parents ever kissing or holding hands in front of me. I *do* remember my parents mocking the mistletoe tradition as "a silly thing to do with a tree parasite."

Ava comes back with two open beer bottles and streams music through the flat screen. Soft jazz pipes into the room through a nice surround sound system. "I stock the refrigerator with essentials when I visit." She hands me a cold one, and we knock bottles.

We sink into the beige suede sofa and drink our beers.

"I've updated the place." Ava kicks off her boots and stretches out on the sofa. Her feet brush against my thigh. "I don't want it to feel like a mausoleum. I want it to be a happy place where I can spend time alone when I want to get out of the city." She eases her feet into my lap. "But honestly, I don't usually visit the neighbors or anyone else when I'm here. I like being with the memories of my family."

Like it's second nature, I rub the top of her foot with my free hand.

"I'm sorry, Rookie." I run my palm over her foot and encircle her slender ankle. "You should've told me. I would've come with you more often."

Shit. Just what I need. I mean, I don't want her to be alone here if she doesn't want to be, but going out of town with her regularly would test any guy's willpower. Especially the guy that's been horny for her for the better part of two years.

I guzzle down a third of my brew.

"You're here now, and that's what counts. I'm ready to share it with someone special, and since Leo isn't an option yet, you're first on my list." She downs more beer without taking her eyes off me.

My chest swells because I'm first on her *Someone Special* list, and she's trusted me with her secret. That's stupid, I know, but then that's my brain around Ava.

She uses a perfectly manicured big toe to stroke circles up my leg until her foot disappears under my jacket. That toe works its way up my abs and across my ribcage.

God. Damn.

I hiss out a breath and stare at the pictures on the mantle. Swear to God, Leo is frowning at me in all of them.

"Want another one?" I ease out of my seat and hope my boner doesn't pop the button on my jeans.

"Sure." Ava's voice is dreamy, and she twists her long ponytail around a finger.

Shit, I want to wrap that ponytail around my fist and bend her over the sofa. Getting another round of beers is a better choice, though, and will buy me some time. I head to the kitchen and hope that when I return, things will be back to normal again. We'll be friends and nothing more.

But deep down, I know I'm lying to myself. Things with Ava can never be the same again after that kiss at her birthday party.

Chapter Nine

I grab two more beers out of the fridge and bring one to Ava. I turn toward the recliner, but she grabs my hand and pushes me toward the seat I just vacated next to her. As soon as my ass connects with the sofa, her sexy-as-fuck foot is on the move again.

"Thanks for coming with me, Dex." She sighs like life couldn't get any better. "I couldn't have done this reunion alone."

Huh. This doesn't sound like the Ava I know. *That* Ava can conquer the world with her razor wit, audacious personality, and million-dollar smile.

"You? The woman who can leap skyscrapers in a single bound. You're saying a small-town high school reunion is your kryptonite?" I laugh.

She flattens her foot against my chest and gives me a playful shove. My hand closes around her foot and holds it there. I caress the soft skin on top. She pulls in a sharp, sexy breath, then the most incredible thing happens—her foot burns a path to the aching bulge in my pants.

My arousal soars to meltdown levels. Chernobyle has nothin' on me. I'm a fucking inferno ready to incinerate both of us and send the house up in flames too. Maybe even the whole fucking county.

"I'm not as tough as I pretend to be," she says all breathy. She slides her beanie off with one hand and tosses it to the floor. "But I do go after the things I want most in life." She shifts, and before I know it, she's reversed her position on the sofa. Her legs are stretched out to the side, and she's leaning over my lap. That full rack that I'd love to see in the buff, brushes against my chest.

I'm certain her lush tits would fit perfectly in the palm of my hand. After I sucked the pink nipples into hard peaks, they'd feel incredible grazing my bare pecs as she rides me to an earth-moving orgasm. She'd cry out my name, and I'd flip her onto her back and pound into her until she comes again. And all the while, she'd murmur my name so we both know who gave her the first real orgasm of her life.

She'd be marked as mine forever.

My grip tightens around the bottle of beer, but the other one seems to have a mind of its own and curls around her hip. If any other pretty woman I was interested in made moves on me like this, I'd already have her undressed and halfway to a screaming orgasm. But this is Ava.

As badly as I want to screw her brains out, I also don't want to fuck up our friendship. I bet the gossip rags wouldn't think I'm such a playboy if they could see me frozen like a scared chess team nerd, unsure of how to handle a woman as gorgeous as Ava, who obviously wants more than friendship at the moment.

She pries the bottle from my hand and sets both hers and mine aside. Her fingers toy with the neckline of my shirt, the tips tracing the edge of my collarbone. "This is nice, you know?" The light scent of brew smooths over my jaw.

Yes, I fucking well know. It's so goddamn nice that I want to peel every stitch of clothing off of you with my teeth.

"Ava, we shouldn't start something we can't finish."

"You said you can keep a secret, right?" Her fingers dip inside the neck of my shirt to caress the spot between my pecs.

I inhale sharp and loud.

"So can I, Dex. This is between you and me, no one else."

I can't help it. I really fucking can't. My hand slides under her sweater to stroke up the length of her spine. She arches into me. Her reaction is so fierce, it leaves no doubt in my dirty mind that she's aroused and ready. No question, she'd respond to my touch if I had all of her clothes off.

"Your brother is always between us, Ava." My voice is scratchy and dry, like I've been chewing cotton.

"Bros before hoes, right?" she smarts off.

My fingers flex into her toned back. "You know that's not what I mean."

She stares at me from under long, silky lashes. "If he's between us, it's because you've put him there."

All the air is sucked from the fucking room when her palm molds around my dick.

"Fuck, Ava."

I don't know if it's me saying *fuck* or me saying it coupled with her name, but her breaths turn quick and shallow. "That's what I'm hoping for," she whispers as she leans in and brushes her lips across mine.

"Ava," I say again, my voice as hard as my prick.

"Don't ruin this, Dex," she murmurs against my lips.

I really wish she wouldn't say my name all sexy and pouty. It makes me want to do exactly what she's asking of me. Exactly what I shouldn't want to do.

"Don't talk unless you're going to say you want to fuck me." Her stare, smoky with desire, anchors to mine. She's waiting. Waiting for me to say it.

My gaze drifts over her flawless face. I caress her cheek with the back of my forefinger, then outline her lips with the pad of my thumb. "You're so fucking beautiful, Ava. Do you know that?"

"But you don't want me." Her tone has gone stony.

That's as far from the truth as a politician's promises during an election year. There's no woman on earth I find more goddamn sexy. No one I want more. No woman I want to fuck but her.

"I'm not just Leo's little sister anymore." Her voice wobbles, and my chest squeezes.

"I know that."

"Do you? I felt like a pathetic, inexperienced little kid next to Cynthia."

"Is that why you were so upset?" I ask. "Because there's no comparison." I sigh. "But you *are* like family, Rookie."

"Really?" She gives me a challenging look. The look that always tells me I'm in trouble. "Would a family member do this?" Her arms lace around my neck, and she lays a smokin' hot kiss on my mouth. It's fast and fierce and frantic like she's been holding back a riptide of desire, and now the breaking waves of lust are flowing and crashing into us.

She tastes like beer and vanilla and sex all rolled into one, and I want her so fucking much it hurts. My arms close around her, tugging her against me. Our breaths are so quick they could break the sound barrier.

My mind is the only part of my body telling me to stop. The rest of my body wants this to happen. All weekend long.

I break the kiss to drag my mouth down the length of her neck. Her scent is as fresh as the autumn air outside, and I breathe her in. Heat pounds through my veins from having her in my arms, having my hands and mouth on her. I want to crawl in bed with her scent every night, wake up with it every morning, and shower with it every day. I'm certain I'd never grow tired of it, and each day I'd just want it all the more. Want her all the more because she's cast a spell on me that can't be broken.

I work her soft earlobe with my teeth and tongue, and sexy little moans and gasps slip through her lips. I imagine her making the same sounds, only louder. Much, much louder because it would be her first real orgasm overtaking her, courtesy of yours truly. It *is* my fucking fantasy so I should be the lucky bastard hovering over her, driving into her until she comes.

She turns her face into my neck and licks the sensitive skin along my collarbone. I groan and pull her tighter against my dick. She feathers kisses up my neck with soft nips and gentle bites along the way until she reaches my ear.

"Dex." Her hot, moist breath against my ear causes a shiver to wash through me. "I'm yours if you want me. I'll do anything, try anything you want. I'm so wet and ready for you."

Jesus fucking Christ. I figure I'm going to hell anyway, but if I teach her the dirty things running through my mind, I'll probably burn twice. Maybe I'm already dead because resisting Ava is pure torment.

"Rookie," I say, and my voice croaks. That's me living up to the suave playboy image. I try to push her away from me so at least her tits won't rub against me and cause my brain to short circuit. Maybe my brain is in slow-mo because in a smooth motion, she's straddling me.

She grinds against my dick. My eyes close. I let out a groan at the incredible friction against my prick. She sinks both hands into my hair and grinds into my cock again. Swear to God, I could spontaneously combust. Then her lips are on mine again, moving and tasting and drinking me in. Her hips and her mouth start to work in unison, and the world around us melts away.

My hand slides under her sweater and finds one of her tits. Her head falls back and she arches, pressing further into my palm. They're as perfect as I knew they would be. I lift the sweater and tug on the low-cut, black satin bra until her breasts plump over the top like a corset.

Fuck, that's such a turn on.

Her nipple is already peaked and straining toward me. I take it between my teeth and bite with just enough pressure for it to sting. She inhales a sharp breath, and her eyes flutter open to look down at me. Our eyes lock as I continue to suck and lick her tender flesh.

Her fingers move furiously through my hair as she stares down at me from under shuttered lashes. Lust glazes over her deep blue eyes, but she doesn't look away. She keeps them locked with mine, watching my mouth work her tender flesh with such erotic movements.

Her hips slide and grind faster. "I've wanted to do this since we kissed at my birthday party," she rasps out.

When I move to the other breast, and close my hot, wet mouth around the peak, she cries out, *"Dex!"*

She rides me faster, exactly the way I imagined she would, sans the clothes.

I release her pebbled nipple and flick my tongue along the soft skin between her tits.

"You can fuck them if you want," she whispers.

Dear God, kill me now. A rush of high-octane lust reaches my lungs and wrings out every drop of air. When I'm with a woman, I'm usually the dirty talker. So far, Ava's got me beat by a few time zones.

My hands fly to her hips. Every time she shifts and grinds, I press her down harder against my throbbing cock.

Best damn dry hump ever.

"Is this your favorite position?" she asks against my lips. "Me on top?"

I want to say so many things. *Every position will be better than the last; I'll make sure of it. We'll try them all until we find your favorite because it won't matter to me as long as I'm with you.*

But I don't say any of those things because I know banging Ava silly will cause problems that I can't handle right now. I think of Leo. I think of what this could do to our friendship and our partnership. To our company. Most of all, I think of what this could do to Ava's bond with her brother.

I grasp her hips firmly to slow her pace. When she finally stills, I say, "Ava." I pull her bra back in place and lower her sweater. "Let's slow down a minute." I lean back, run a set of fingers through my hair, and adjust my glasses.

Shit, my glasses haven't fogged up like this since the night I lost my v-card at a college frat party. Being a member of the chess team, I wasn't a regular, but I happened to land an invitation because I tutored several of the fraternity brothers that semester. It was fucking hot and steamy in the frat house laundry room. Especially since the girl that so generously relieved me of my virginity was sitting on the dryer and it was set to "High."

Ava's forehead wrinkles, and her blue eyes dim to a smoky gray. Then she smiles and slides off my lap. "Well, at least we got a little more *comfortable* with each other before tonight. We should have no problem pulling off the lie that we're a couple."

Slowly, I stand, because this boner isn't going away any time soon unless I have a few minutes alone in the shower. Speaking of...

"Why don't we go find the hotel and get settled in," I say. I don't care what reservations Ava made; I'm requesting different floors when we check-in. The more distance between us the better.

"Oh." Her lips form a circle, and my mind blanks for a sec. Because I can't help but picture those lips forming the same shape around my cock.

Goddammit. Get a fucking grip, Moore.

Yeah, definitely need a long shower and soap to lube up my hand. It's the only way I'll be able to step out in public tonight without embarrassing myself.

"We're staying here at the house all weekend," Ava says, and I know I'm fucking doomed.

Chapter Ten

Ava uses the master bathroom on the far end of the house to get cleaned up and leaves the bathroom down the hall to me. I turn on the shower so I can get ready for the alumni party where I'll act as Ava's date. A dating couple usually holds hands. They touch. They kiss. No way can I manage that with a raging hard-on.

I let the steam build while I bring up iTunes on my phone and play some rock and roll. Perfect noise for cover. When I jerk off, I'm usually alone in my apartment because porn babes don't count. But this is different. I'm desperate to do something so I can make it through the night without taking what Ava has offered.

While Def Leppard sings *Pour Some Sugar On Me*, I get in the shower and try to dial up the mental image of the last good lay I've had. I'm not a douche. Every woman I'm with knows the score right up front—my job comes first, and I'm not ready to settle down. I've dated some beautiful women, but no one comes to mind but Ava.

On to plan B. I try to remember the last time I watched a dirty movie. *Aaaand* still nothing. Except Ava's beautiful, fuckable tits in my mouth.

Note to self: watch more porn. You never know when it might come in handy. Like now, because I need to get what just happened between me and Ava out of my system before I can go out in public.

A Guns N' Roses tune echoes off the walls of the small bathroom as I rack my brains to find a muse. I wash my hair and soap up my body. My hand slides over the Checkmate logo tattooed on my ribcage. I realize Ava's never seen my ink. She knows it's there, though, because she designed it. My sudsy hand lingers over the black knight chess piece. A stallion, its mane flowing as if it's in a full gallop. The word *Checkmate Inc.*

artistically angles through the base.

Me, Oz, and Leo were still dumbass punks when we started the company, and back then I still thought of Ava as Leo's kid sister. She was already showing talent for computer graphics, so Leo asked her to design our logo. On our way to celebrate with tequila shots, we stumbled across a parlor called *Tattoo Charlie's*. Since we were each getting the same tattoo, Charlie himself suggested we choose different locations on our bodies. He said three dudes getting the same tat in the same spot wouldn't be *cool*. Guess the glasses gave away our inner geekster.

Or maybe it was the Star Trek shirts. No idea which.

The water streams over me, and my fingertip traces the outline of the tat. Riding her to her very first real climax has been playing through my filthy mind. I keep thinking it would mark her as mine, something else besides the nickname that she only shares with me. But now the tables are turned, and I can't help but feel like I'm the one that's marked.

It's not just the tat. Her mouth on mine, her hand cupping my dick, her dirty words...they've all marked me. No other woman turns me on like she does.

My dick throbs harder. I can't help it. Finally, I give in to the images I've been trying to fight off for days. Ava completely naked. Better to fantasize about it than to act on it, right? I soap up my hand and wrap it around my shaft. I close my eyes and let my head tilt back as my hand starts to work its magic. Truth is, Ava *is* my muse. How fitting, since she named her web design firm 5 Muse Designs. That can't be a coincidence.

I take her up on her offer and slide my swollen cock into the deep valley between her tits. She's sitting on the edge of my bed, and I'm standing in front of her. Both of her hands mold around the sides of her breasts to push them tight around my shaft. Her manicured nails curl over the top of those luscious tits.

And hell fucking yeah, her nails are painted cherry fuck-me red to match the heavy lipstick she's wearing. It *is* a fantasy, after all. I might as well add black stockings and a garter belt too.

I let that picture form in my mind.

Oh hell yeah. Go big or go home.

My grip tightens and picks up speed, and I pretend it's my hips pumping up and down between her tits. The water slides over me, keeping my skin moist and slick. The first ache of orgasm burgeons somewhere deep in my core and spreads through my limbs. My muscles flex and tense, and I brace my free hand against the shower wall.

In my fantasy, my fingers slide into her silky hair as my hips thrust harder. My skin is on fire, and I don't know if it's the hot water or the flames of lust burning through me. Ava's not a rookie in my fantasy. She's confident and sexy and beautiful as fuck as her gaze locks with mine, and she smiles up at me. I'm about to drop to my knees and sink my tongue into her pussy because I'm certain it's wet with arousal and ready for me to take her. But my fantasy acquires a mind of its own, and Ava dips her head, wraps those red painted lips around my swollen dick and begins to fuck me with her mouth.

Eddie Van Halen rips through the chords of *Eruption* as release crashes into me, tearing a muffled noise of satisfaction from deep in my chest.

Long live rock and roll.

I brace both hands against the shower wall with the water pounding onto my chest, my neck, my face. It takes a few minutes, but my breathing returns to normal, and I feel like I can think with the right head again.

Fifteen minutes later, I'm dressed in Tom Ford from head to toe. Black custom-fitted pants, matching vest, white dress shirt cuffed up my forearms, and a tie. No matching jacket. Just a black wool pea coat, which is slung over the sofa arm until we leave. I slick back my damp hair so it doesn't hang in my face, and the length barely grazes my collar. I pace the length of the den and wait for Ava to finish getting ready.

Ava's heels click against the wood floor, and I turn to greet her. Only I can't speak because she's so fucking gorgeous. Her hair is swept up in a bundle of curls, a few strategic strands hang loose around her face and neck. Diamond teardrops dangle from her ears, and the only other jewelry she's wearing are the bracelets I gave her. She's wearing a red satin halter dress. Yes *that* red. The one that colored her nails and lips in my imagination a few minutes ago. The dress flows and flirts around the lower part of her thighs. But the mouth-watering icing on the Ava cake is going to be the death of me. The front dips ridiculously low between her breasts to reveal the valley I recently fucked in my shower fantasy.

She hands me a black velvet overcoat. "Can you help me, please?"

She turns around, and I help her slide into the fine fabric. It's all I can do not to rake my lips from her bare shoulder all the way to the nape of her neck and then place an openmouthed kiss right below the knot that's holding her dress together.

"Thanks." She faces me and buttons her coat. "You look nice, by the way. How was your shower?"

I nearly choke. I scrub a hand across my jaw to mask my guilt.

"Good," I say. "It was really hot." I cough. "Nice. The hot water was nice."

And didn't do a damn bit of good because I still want her. In nothing but that sexy velvet coat, the bracelets, and those heels with her legs spread wide open to welcome me in.

She hooks the last button and stares up at me with shining eyes and shimmering lips. "Are you ready?"

Fucking hell, am I ever.

"Yeah," I grunt out. My superior vocabulary is alive and well.

"Great," Ava says, and heads to the door. With one hand on the doorknob, she tosses a look over a velvety shoulder. "And Dex?"

I try to peel my eyes off her toned calves. "Huh?" Really, my mastery of the English language is astounding.

"I know it's going to be difficult since I'm such a *sister* to you, but you're supposed to be my date." She manages to smile, but not a hint of it shows in her icy eyes. She's angry. Or hurt. Or both. "Maybe you could...oh, I don't know...pretend to find me attractive. We have to act like we're fucking, even though we're not."

Ava pushes through the door, and the screen falls shut with a *thwack, thwack, thwack*. The click of her heels grows dim as she steps off the porch and walks to my car.

I know I've fucked up. Jacking off while fantasizing about Ava has only made me want her more. That dress isn't helping to tame my dirty thoughts or my desire for her either. Truth is, I'm screwed one way or the other.

Chapter Eleven

Ava and I are fashionably late to the homecoming reunion. After a kid wearing a student senate badge takes our coats, we find our way to the school gym where the party is already in full swing. The music is loud, and the room is already heating up from so many people.

The gym has seen better days, but it's decked out with purple, silver, and white streamers. School spirit is splashed on every wall with banners that say "Monarch Pride!" A fierce lion wearing a crown that tilts to one side of its flowing mane is the mascot, and large, intimidating paw prints mark a path on all four walls.

We make our way toward the refreshments, and I let Ava take the lead. She tries to weave through the ocean of people. It seems impossible, and she comes to a halt in front of a wall of alums. I bump into her from behind, and searing heat burns my skin everywhere we're touching.

Someone backs into us, laughing. I curl my fingers around Ava's hip to steady her. Her fingers tighten around mine, and for a second, she leans back into me. We both stop breathing.

She releases my hand abruptly. "Wait here. I'll get the punch."

I'm tall, so I can see over the crowd. It parts as she weaves a path through it to the refreshments table.

Two men with red, puffy eyes and obnoxious facial expressions are obviously a few sheets to the wind and blocking the punch bowl. Ava maneuvers around them and pours us two glasses of purple punch.

Jealousy rushes through me as the two drunken asshats turn to check her out, not even trying to hide their leers. I push through the crowd until I'm standing a few feet behind Ava. I shove my hands in my pockets and wait. I don't have the right to act like a jealous boyfriend, even if I'm supposed to be her date tonight.

Asshat Number One withdraws a flask from his jacket and leans over to speak to her in a drunken whisper that's louder than the DJ's music. "It's better with a splash of this." He snorts with laughter.

She's startled but gives him a quick, polite smile. "No thanks."

Asshat Number One is either too drunk or too stupid to take a hint. "Jordan Winthrop." He extends his hand, invading Ava's personal space.

I take a step closer but restrain the urge to wrap my arms around her from behind.

Asshat Number One is tall—big enough to have been a jock back in the day—but now he's packed on thirty or so extra pounds, which hangs over his cheap, cheesy belt. I, on the other hand, have packed on at least that amount of muscle since my high school days.

"Yes, I remember you," Ava says, and shakes his hand. He doesn't let go right away, and she pulls it free. This time her smile isn't so polite. In fact, she's not smiling at him at all.

I want to teach this guy some manners, and I definitely won't let him get away with much more rudeness. But I know Ava. If I step in too soon, she'll insist she could've managed on her own. So I wait for just the right moment by studying her. I'm so tuned into her I'll know the exact moment when the hardness of her stare and the strain around her mouth shifts.

Plus, seeing her bring this asshole to his knees like I know she can will be entertaining. Ava is no shrinking violet.

"Really?" Asshat Number One slurps his drink. "I don't recall ever meeting you."

Ava keeps that smile in place, like it's cemented on. "We went to school together from sixth grade until tenth grade," she deadpans, and picks up both glasses of punch from the table.

"Were you in sports?" Asshat Number Two asks. He snaps his fingers. "Or a cheerleader?"

"Brendan." Ava stiffens. She so obviously dislikes Asshat Number Two even more than his friend. Her lips part, and I smile to myself because I know that razor sharp wit of hers is about to shave the stupid smiles right off of Team Asshat's faces.

Before she can respond, a nice-looking brunette walks up to Asshat Number One and slides an arm around his shoulders. They're obviously together. She's followed by a bleached blonde. Both are attractive, well dressed, and probably cheerleader material once upon a time. They give Ava a predatory stare like she's encroaching on their territory.

"Don't be silly, Jordan," the brunette says. "Ava was on the *science* team." It's so obviously meant as an insult.

Heated anger singes every one of my nerve endings because I remember what it was like to be mocked for being smart. I just never considered that Ava had been through the same thing. She's so attractive and funny, and her brilliance only makes her more gorgeous in my eyes.

"Tiffany," Ava says, like the word scares her. "Gee, um."

I'm stunned. Ava's boldness has vanished. She tries to back away from the bullies, but her bottom goes up against the table and stops her.

I can't stay out of it any longer. I close the space between us, take a glass of punch from Ava's hand, and pull her close. "Thanks, sweetheart."

Her eyes flare with something I can't quite put a name to. Maybe it's gratitude. Maybe it's longing.

"Hi, babe," she says back.

When she calls me *babe*, I graze a soft, lingering kiss across her lips, careful not to smudge her sexy red lipstick. It seems like the most natural thing, to be kissing Ava like she's my girl.

She snuggles into my side. "Everyone, this is Dex Moore."

Asshat One and Two mumble a greeting. Tiffany scrutinizes both Ava and me, and I can't tell if Mean Girl is thinking we're both nerds who belong together or if she can tell we're faking it.

"Jordan and Tiffany were the dream couple in high school," Ava says to me. "Homecoming king and queen, head cheerleader, captain of the basketball team. Everyone knew they'd get married one day."

"Six years now," Jordan says, looking very proud he landed a trophy wife.

Tiffany doesn't seem quite as impressed with her prize. "It's seven years, honey."

"Two kids, and she still looks great, doesn't she?" Jordan pulls his wife close with a clumsy tug. She wobbles on her skyscraper heels.

That's when I notice Blondie, Tiffany's friend, eyeballing me like a hungry shark and I'm the catch of the day. I clear my throat and ignore her, but she doesn't want to be ignored.

"You look familiar," Blondie says to me while totally ignoring Ava. She still hasn't acknowledged Ava's presence.

"Can't imagine why." I take a drink of punch.

Blondie keeps studying me until her eyes flair with recognition.

Shit.

"You're one of the partners of Checkmate Inc. Your CEO went to high school here." She glances at Ava and sniffs, then turns her attention back on me. "I saw an interview of you three not long ago. Kept up with all the press." I swear her voice is almost a growl of lust. "I'm a reporter for the Albany Times." She looks at Ava again.

"Suzanna," Ava greets Blondie.

Blondie's greeting is a mere nod. "I think I remember you."

Ava flashes her a million-dollar smile. "I definitely remember you. Mrs. Franks had me tutor you in biology because you were failing."

I have to cough behind my hand to keep from snorting punch through my nose.

Blondie's smile turns evil. I half expect her to put a curse on us and fly from the room on a broomstick.

"You moved away during high school, right?" Blondie says. "Because of some sort of accident."

There has to be a special place in hell for people like Suzanna. Ava's parents were killed. A tragedy of that magnitude must've ripped through a town this size, and all Blondie remembers is there was some sort of accident? Either that or she's so cold and callous she doesn't care what such a tragedy must've done to her classmate.

"My decision to move to the city instead of Leo moving back to Weatherton was based more on the people here." Ava keeps a cool, steady gaze on Blondie, who narrows her eyes. "And because I wanted Leo to have his dream. He earned it."

A switch flips on in the back of my mind. Leo didn't make Ava move to the city. She chose to. Both because she didn't fit in here for being a brainiac, and because she didn't want Leo to put his life on hold for her. So she moved to New York City, and he put her in a swanky school for the intellectually gifted where she could finally be a "normal" kid. The bond between them ran so deep, even back then that they were both willing to give up their whole lives for each other in the wake of losing their parents.

My parents didn't even help me move into the dorms when I picked Columbia over Princeton. I can't be the jerk that gets between Ava and Leo after all they've been through. Hell, I can't even understand the kind of selfless connection they have.

I'm about to pull Ava away when the music stops. A fifty-something woman with thick glasses walks up on stage with a microphone. "Welcome home, Monarch Alums!"

The crowd cheers.

"I'm Principal Franks, and it's time to start our auction. Thank you to all the alumni who so generously donated the items we'll be auctioning off tonight. All the money raised will go to building a new gymnasium for the next generation of Monarchs, so it's for a very worthy cause."

More cheers round the gym.

Several items are auctioned off from local businesses, most of the owners obviously having grown up here. A gift certificate for plumbing services. Unconventional, but okay. Everybody needs a good plumber once in a while. Handmade jewelry from a small boutique. Nice. A set of braces from an orthodontist in the next town over. And many more items that all go to the highest bidders.

"I saved the best for last." Principal Franks beams at Ava. "I wish the school could afford to bid on it because we need this particular item. It's a custom website design package from our very own Ava Foxx. Ava is the chief designer and a founding partner of 5 Muse Designs, one of the fastest growing web design firms in New York City. This package has a retail value of ten thousand dollars, folks, so dig deep and let the bidding begin!"

Ooooos and *ahhhhs* ripple through the crowd.

Jordan lifts his finger to bid on it, which elicits a subtle glare from his wife. Since Jordan is drunk off his ass, he doesn't notice. "My used car lot needs a professional website," he slurs.

A used car salesman. Why am I not surprised?

His wife crosses her arms over her chest and sulks.

The bidding continues until Jordan reaches the insulting amount of two thousand dollars, and the bids stop rolling in. Principal Franks looks crestfallen. Ava doesn't, and I know why. She couldn't care less how little her services go for. Her heart is so big she'll do the same quality job for a two-thousand-dollar client as she will for a ten-thousand-dollar client, then she'll turn around and donate more cash for the gymnasium. That's just the way she rolls.

Principal Franks says, "Going once...going twice..."

Oh, hell no. No way am I going to let Asshat Number One walk away with Ava's services, especially not at such a degrading price.

"Fifty thousand dollars." The words tumble out of my mouth without a second thought.

The entire gymnasium gasps at once, including Ava. She turns big, round eyes on me, and they're filled with so much emotion that it plucks at the strings of my heart.

Silence settles over the crowd, and Principal Franks' jaw is hanging so far open she could catch flies in it. "Uh, are there any other bids?" she finally manages.

I ignore Jordan's and Tiffany's disdainful looks over being dethroned. Blondie is giving me the evil eye too. Not sure what her problem is, other than she never grew past the high school mean-girl phase.

"Going, once, twice, three times. Sold for fifty thousand dollars to the gentleman in the vest!" Principal Franks shouts so fast, like she's afraid I might change my mind. "Sir, can we get your name?"

"Uh." I clear my throat. "Dex Moore."

The crowd buzzes with whispers and murmurs.

I discard our punch cups onto the refreshments table and take Ava's hand. I tug her through the crowd to meet Principal Franks as she walks off the stage, and the DJ cranks up another tune.

"Ms. Franks, I don't need a new website. I've already got the best site and the best designer in the state working for my company." I nod at Ava. "So I'm donating the package to the school."

Principal Franks pumps my hand like I've just handed her a gold mine. I guess fifty grand in cash and a free website *is* like striking gold for a public school in a small town. There's never enough money to provide everything the kids need.

"Ava, it's clear you've made your mark on the world," Principal Franks says.

Those words blow me away. Ava *has* made her mark. On me.

"And you've obviously made very wise decisions in your career and your personal associations. You're both very generous, and you look like a couple who is very much in love."

Chapter Twelve

Ava and I are completely alone in a gymnasium full of people. Principal Franks has moved on, and the music is so loud I can barely think.

Ava leans in close, and her lips brush across my ear. "Is it true?"

"Is what true?" I pretend I don't know what she's talking about. But I so fucking do. She wants to know if her old principal's deduction is spot on. She's asking me if I'm in love with her. I don't want to answer the question. I'm not sure I can admit the truth to myself.

This is where Ava would typically give me an eye roll as big as a skyscraper. Or tap her knuckles gently against my head.

She doesn't do either this time. Instead, she stares up at me, chewing her bottom lip with anticipation.

"Of course I love you," I say, and her breath hitches.

Shit, I can't do this. I can't lead her on, so I quickly add, "I love you and Leo both. And Oz too, even though he's an ass sometimes." My joke doesn't hit home, and she steps back. She looks up at me with misty eyes and a quivering lip. It's like someone has taken a laser, inserted it into my chest, and carved out my heart because I'm sure it's not beating anymore.

I reach for her hand, but she backs away and rushes from the gym.

I go after her. When I step through the gym doors, the tap of her heels echoes through the empty hallway. I follow the sound down the hall and turn right just as she crashes through the front door of the school.

I lengthen my strides to catch up. When I finally reach her, she's leaning against the hood of my Porsche, breathing heavily.

The parking lot is dotted with trees, and my car is parked

under one of them. Not all of the autumn leaves have fallen, so the streetlights filter through to dance over Ava. I approach slowly so she won't run away from me again.

"Ava, I'm in a tough spot here. What do you want me to say?" My lungs tighten so much I can hardly breathe.

"I want you to tell me the truth, Dex. Why did you bid such an obscene amount on a website you don't need, then donate it back to a school you didn't attend?" Her arms are wrapped around her center, and she's shivering because she left her coat inside.

I don't have a jacket to offer her this time, so I step into her and wrap her in my arms. She fists my vest in both hands.

"Because I can afford it, and the school needs it." I'm being a douche for avoiding the whole truth. I know it. Ava knows it. The fucking street lamp knows it, so I fess up. "And because I couldn't let those asshat classmates of yours take advantage of your hard work. They didn't deserve you back in high school, and they certainly don't deserve you now."

That's the truth. Mostly.

"That was pretty great." Her soft words feather across my cheeks.

"What's the story with Tiffany and her band of merry asshats?" I can guess, but I want to know what Ava is thinking.

She shrugs. "Brendan..."

"Asshat Number Two."

She snorts. "That's the one. Well, I'd never been on a date, and he asked me out. He was popular, you know? And so I said yes, but then I found out he just wanted me to help him pass biology." Her voice shakes with humiliation, and I want to protect her the same way Leo does. "So I canceled the date, but he told everyone that he stood me up because I was a nobody. And now they don't even remember me. That's how insignificant I was back then."

"Ava, the last thing you could ever be is insignificant." I press a kiss into her hair.

"I'm so glad I never went out with Brendan. Right before I moved, he was arrested for mooning old ladies from the front on a dare."

"So he's a perv?" I ask.

Ava shrugs. "Either that or just stupid. I mean, who takes a dare like that in a town this size? Did he think they wouldn't recognize him? His grandmother lived in the nursing home where he flashed those little old ladies." Ava's snorting laughter gets louder. "And he didn't wear a mask to cover his face."

"Jesus, what a dumbass." I laugh along with her.

"Thank you for what you did in there." She nods toward the gym. "It was so sweet, and it made me feel so special."

And that answers the rest of her question. The one truth I can't bring myself to fully form into words because of what it might cost her. "You *are* special to me, Ava. Don't you know that by now?"

She slides her flattened hand up my chest, and the bracelets I gave her jingle. "Sometimes I'm more sure of it than anything in the world." Her voice quivers, but she levels those intense blue eyes at me. The street light glints off of them. Her other hand slips under my vest and caresses my abs. They tense and release under her touch.

"Ava." Her name rushes out on a heated breath.

"And then we get close...like this, and you pull away."

She slips two fingers between the buttons of my dress shirt, and I hiss out a breath that's part pleasure and part torture.

"I can't pretend not to have feelings for you anymore, Dex. I want to know the truth about how you really feel about me." Her clever fingers free a button from its hole, and she slips her whole hand inside my shirt.

I grind my teeth into dust, trying to hold on to my sanity. I don't think I can resist this pull between us much longer. I want her so fucking much. Right here. Right now.

I realize my grip on her has tightened, and one hand has dropped so far south I should be speaking a foreign language.

"No more avoiding the subject." Her stubborn determination—you know, the one I claim to love so much—isn't so loveable at the moment because it's backing me into a corner.

Her hand slides dangerously low on my bare abs. My mind blanks, but my dick stands at attention and gives her a twenty-one gun salute. It's totally not fair for her to ask me these kinds of questions with her hand on the move and about to breach the hot zone. I try to speak, but I'm so turned on that it comes out sort of like a grunt.

"I want to know how you really feel about me, Dex." Her hand drops to my dick, and she cups me.

I come apart at the fucking seams.

My hands glide down the outside of her thighs until my fingertips find the hem of her dress. She draws in a sharp breath and holds it while my searching hands inch up her bare legs to cup her ass.

The panty gods have chosen to smile on me, because she's wearing a thong.

I groan, and devour those sexy red lips with mine. They part and I don't just slip through. I invade her with a hot, hungry tongue. She squeaks when my palms close around the cheeks of her ass and I lift her onto the hood of my car.

My hands are still cupped under her ass, and I position her on the edge of my car. "This is how I feel about you." I step between her legs and hold her against my aching dick. She lets out a muffled scream against my shoulder when I grind my hard-on against her pussy. My pants and the thin layer of lace between us aren't enough of a barrier to mask the heat where we connect.

"Tell me more," she rasps out, her face buried in the crook of my neck.

"I've wanted to fuck you for two long years," I say as I grind another sexy gasp out of her. "I want to fuck you every way possible." Every time I drop the F-bomb, she arches into me, and her pussy gets hotter against my dick. "Fast, slow, hard, soft." My words get dirtier with each sentence, and Ava gets more turned on.

She's trembling in my arms and keeps her face nestled against my neck and shoulder. I circle my hips again and crush her against my prick.

"Oh, Dex." She grabs my shoulders to steady herself, and her nails curl into my flesh with just enough sting to turn me on even more.

I think I hear the crunch of gravel, but I can't be sure. Ava's heavy breathing and cries of ecstasy drown out everything else in my world. I still and listen just in case, look over a shoulder, but no one is there.

So I turn my lips back to her ear and keep whispering the filthiest things. I'm all in now, and there's no going back. "I'm so fucking glad no one else has made that hot little pussy of yours come, because I'm going to be the first. You're going to come so hard and so many times you'll lose count."

She's whimpering now as I slide a hand between her legs and rub. Her panties are hot and moist, and she shivers so hard at my touch that she's practically convulsing in my arms.

I don't kiss her. I don't pull back to look into her eyes. I keep my lips next to her ear, softly grazing across it so that my heated breath and the wisps of her hair tickle her skin. It works because another tremble racks through her hot body.

The strip of lace covering her pussy grows wetter with each stroke. "Do you want me to *fuck* you, Ava?" I'll give in to my lust for her just this once. Just for this weekend. And live on the memory of sharing her first real orgasm for the rest of my life.

"*Yes.*" She swallows. "Yes, *please.*"

I chuckle against her throat and bite into the soft flesh there just enough for it to sting.

She hisses in a breath.

"I like it when you beg," I murmur, and nip at her earlobe. "At your birthday party, you begged me to take you to the reunion. You have no idea how badly I wanted to bend you over and take you the way you *need* to be taken right there on the balcony."

"That..." She's panting so hard, she's half delirious. "That would've been lovely."

"*Lovely?*" I say with a mocking laugh. "Sweetheart, lovely isn't the word you're going to use when we're done, I guarantee it."

"What word will I use?"

"'Big' comes to mind." I chuckle.

Her hands slide to my belt and go to work on the buckle like she can't wait to get started.

Uneasiness coasts through me. Fucking Ava is one thing. Fucking her in public where anyone can catch us in the act is another. I look over my shoulder again, but we're still alone.

When she has my pants open, I push her hands aside. "Not yet, Rookie." Goddamn, I don't know if I can last when she finally touches me.

"I don't want to be a rookie anymore." She looks up at me with big eyes. They're so open and honest, and I know she's not talking about the reason I gave her that name so many years ago. She's talking about finding that elusive orgasm that she's never had the pleasure of experiencing.

I trace her jawline with the pad of my thumb. "Tonight's your last night as a rookie," I promise. "At least when it comes to orgasms."

"What if I can't?" she asks, fear lacing her words.

I place a finger under her chin and lift her gaze to mine. "You're not the problem." I drop a hot, wet, openmouthed kiss on her and then gaze deep into her eyes. "The problem is you've yet to sleep with a guy who knows what he's doing between the sheets."

She swallows hard. "If you're trying to convince me that you're the guy who knows how to fuck me the right way, it's not necessary. You pretty much had me at 'big.'" She wraps her legs around my hips and locks her ankles to my ass.

I dip two fingers inside her panties and smooth them along her slick entrance. Her uncontrollable shimmy sets my already tingling skin on fire.

"I bet you taste so fucking good." I keep the dirty talk going. She thinks the F-bomb is sexy, so I drop it a few more times. "Do you want me to fuck you with my tongue, Ava?" Works like a charm.

"*Yes.*" Her head falls back, and her long lashes brush the creamy skin under her eyes.

"And my cock?" I tease her.

"*God, yes.*" Her eyes are still closed.

Her sex is soaking my fingertips as I keep stroking her heated pussy. I uncurl one of her hands from my shoulder and place it on the hood.

"Lean back and enjoy the ride, sweetheart." She braces herself with both arms behind her, and I sink two fingers into her wet heat.

A deep throaty cry of pleasure rips from her. That drives me on, and I withdraw my fingers, then pump them into her again. Her scream splits the air around us. My hand picks up speed, and she writhes and squirms with each thrust. She's close. I know she is by the tension rippling through her. I find her throbbing clit with my thumb and circle it while I keep fucking her with my fingers. I slide as deep inside of her as I can and curl my index finger into her pulsing pussy.

Bingo. That thrust and curl move hits her G-spot, and she explodes into a window-shattering orgasm. Her muscles contract and convulse around my fingers, and I massage deep inside of her to prolong the climax. She's soaring above the clouds, and just so there's no goddamn mistaking that I can bring her more pleasure with just two fingers than any other man or machine, I curl those two fingers into her G-spot again.

She screams in pleasure and clamps her arms around my shoulders to hang on for dear life while she rides the wave of orgasm that's cresting at her core. I bury my face in her neck, and pull her close until she descends from the clouds.

I swear I hear the crunch of gravel again and a faint laugh. I still and shelter Ava in my embrace, hoping my broad shoulders will hide her. Of course, it's a little hard to protect her from embarrassment with her legs clamped around my ass and my unzipped pants drooping like a gangbanger.

There's nothing but silence in the darkness, so I brush it off as paranoia. And maybe a little guilt. I've always known that if I ever opened this door with Ava, I wouldn't be able to close it again, and that scares the hell out of me.

I zip my pants and buckle my belt. Then I help her down from the hood. "Get in." I open the car door for her. "I'll get our coats and be right back."

Before I can close the door, she fists my vest and pulls me down for a kiss. It's soft but sensual with tongue. Lots and lots of tongue. I let her take the lead on this one because it's really fucking nice after what we just shared.

As she deepens the kiss, I mold a palm to her cheek. The kiss goes on for a long time, and our breaths kick up a notch. We're both getting turned on again.

Finally, I break the kiss before I do her again right here in the parking lot.

"Thank you," she says, and I know she's talking about her first orgasm without double A batteries. Courtesy of yours truly. Fuck the Energizer bunny. That little bastard can piss off.

My nose brushes hers. "We're not done yet, Rookie."

Not by a long shot.

Chapter Thirteen

Ava is all over me during the drive back to her house. Swear to God, I have to lock her hand in mine to keep her from giving me a hand job all the way home.

Not that I'd mind. I'm one hundred and fifty percent certain I'd enjoy the hell out of it. My first concern is Ava, though. I want her to be thoroughly satisfied before we start acting out *my* fantasies.

"Come on." She leans over the console and kisses my neck. Her hair has escaped from its clip and falls across my chest. "Live dangerously."

I tug her hand to my lips and feather a kiss along the side of her finger. "Having sex on the hood of my car in the parking lot of your old high school during a school function isn't dangerous enough for you?"

"No, it's not, since I didn't get to return the favor. Yet."

Christ Almighty, I want to give her full access to the plank of wood in my pants, but we're just a few minutes from her house. Instead, I slip her fingertip between my lips and suck.

A sharp breath whistles through her lips.

When I pull into the drive and park, she's already got both of our seatbelts undone and is trying to go down on me. That boldness is what I love about her. The way she tackles everything, holds nothing back like it might be her last chance in life to do so. She's obviously going to take the same approach to sex.

"Ava," I say through gritted teeth. I crack the car door, so the inside light flickers to life, but she ignores me. So I wind that beautiful, flowing hair around my hand and tug her mouth up to mine. I lay a deep, demanding kiss on her so she knows I'm in charge. When I finally disentangle my tongue from hers, her baby blues are glazed with so much hunger it knocks the wind from my lungs.

I'm on fire and wound so tight I could blow at any second.

"Round two is happening inside, sweetheart." I give her silky locks another tug, so her head is angled back and her neck is exposed. I place a hot, openmouthed kiss on the soft flesh and suckle. "Car sex will have to wait," I murmur against her throat.

She swallows and rasps out, "Not too long I hope. I'm dying to know what you taste like."

I keep biting and sucking and kissing her creamy skin. "I didn't say tasting had to wait." I kiss my way across her jawline to the corner of her mouth. "You can suck my dick tonight." I bite her bottom lip, and she gasps at my deliciously filthy talk. "After I fuck an orgasm out of you."

Before I can stop her, she climbs over the console into my lap. Our weight pushes the cracked door wide open, and we tumble onto the drive, laughing.

I help her up, and we're practically having sex while walking. We're connected everywhere. Our hands and lips are desperately roaming over each other all the way to the door. No idea how we get inside the house with our clothes still on, but we do, and she's trying to climb me like a tree as soon as the door slams shut.

"Hold up, Rookie." I wrap my arms around her and tighten my grip until she stills.

"You..." She swallows, and disappointment threads through her tone. The lamp she left on shimmers off her searching eyes. "You're not changing your mind, are you?"

Fuck no. I'm a goddamn locomotive steaming down the tracks with so much momentum that nothing can stop this from happening. "'Course not, but there's a couple things I need to say first."

She stares up at me, waiting for me to finish.

"If you change your mind at any time, all you have to do is say so," I say. "Understood?"

She nods. "What else?"

I brush a sultry kiss across her lips. "Since this is going to be your first orgasm with me inside you, I'm calling the shots." My lips sweep across hers again. "We can do things your way tomorrow."

Her eyelids slide shut, and she whispers, "'Kay."

I brush a strand of hair off her cheek and frame her face with both of my hands. She's so beautiful. So sexy.

So mine.

My chest expands and contracts.

I'm about to fuck Ava. I'm about to walk through a door that will change our relationship forever. Anticipation fills me, but so does doubt. It's too late, though. Our kiss on the balcony rocked my foundation, and it's crumbled a little more with each touch, each kiss. It's a pile of rubble after finger fucking her on my car. Even if I back out now, there's no going back to the way things have always been between us. Not completely.

I'm so fucking not backing out, anyway. The only direction is forward, and I'm in overdrive.

Her eyes flutter open as I stare down at her.

"You're so goddamn beautiful I could stare at you all night," I whisper. "The only thing I can imagine even coming close right now is you naked." All dirty talk is forgotten, and I'm baring my soul to the person I trust most in the world. The person I care about most.

"Should I undress, or do you want to take my clothes off?" she asks.

"Every stitch is mine." Excitement hums through me. I trace the edge of her halter dress over a shoulder and work the knot loose at the nape of her neck.

Before the strips of red silk fall free, I mold my palms over her breasts and massage. I know the smooth fabric will create just enough friction to drive her wild.

She moans. Her breaths quicken, and her gaze fills with

the thrill of things I've promised. When her nipples are hard pebbles, I let the red silk slide away. Her perky tits greet me, and the dirtiest thoughts spiral through my mind. But what causes pride to swell in my chest is the fact that this gorgeous woman, who is as smart as she is sexy, is all mine.

At least for now.

I skim the back of my fingers across her taut nipples, and she lets out a sexy sound of approval. I've got a long list of things I want to do to these beautiful babies, and not just for my pleasure. I want to please Ava in so many ways, starting with these luscious breasts. I plan to spend so much time with them they'll ache with both pleasure and need.

I nuzzle the sensitive skin behind her ear and drag my lips down to the nook of her neck. When my mouth slides to the rise of her breast, a shiver glides over her. I kiss and tongue my way to the valley between and lick.

Her head falls back, and she sinks all ten fingers into my hair.

I smile against her skin. It's hot from my touch, and her heart is beating so hard I can feel her racing pulse against my lips. My hands find the zipper at her back, and I ease it down inch by agonizing inch. I know by her murmurs that it's just as much torture for her as it is for me, and that's my goal. I don't want to rush this. Rushing things in the sack isn't my style. Especially not with Ava.

It's so damn good that I want to savor every second of it. But mostly, I want *her* to experience every sensation. I want to draw it out, prolong the moment, so her body sings with anticipation and pleasure.

The zipper purrs as it slowly descends. As soon as it opens at her hips, the fuck-me red dress that's had my hard-on raging all night slips to the floor with a swoosh. She steps out of it, and I'm speechless all over again. She's braless, and her body is pure perfection. Even more beautiful than I've imagined. Okay, even more beautiful than I've *fantasized*, but we don't need to get literal with vocabulary at a time like this.

A small swatch of red lace covers the Promised Land, and I groan just looking at her. She's wearing nothing else but heels, earrings, and the bracelets I gave her. I want those high heels clamped to my ass again, or even better, to my shoulders.

My gaze travels from the top of her honey-colored hair to the tips of her siren red toes. My hungry stare slides and glides over her. Lust burns through me so hot that I loosen the tie knotted at my throat and flick open the top button of my shirt. I know my desire is apparent, mostly because I'm not trying to hide it. I want her to see what she does to me.

Satisfaction flickers in her eyes at my appraisal, and the tension in her shoulders relaxes.

I lift a single index finger and spin it in a circle.

Slowly, sensually, Ava turns in a circle.

And oh. My. Fucking. God.

No lie, my vision blurs.

Her back is to me, the strip of lace disappearing between her perfectly rounded ass cheeks. It reappears just above the dimples over each cheek and stretches around her nice hips. She's not scary skinny, just curved in all the right places.

I growl like a fucking animal and close the gap between us in one long stride.

"I'm going to slide my tongue and my fingers over every inch of you," I say in a hungry whisper as I capture her mouth with mine.

She trembles in my arms.

I mold a palm to her hip, and my other hand slips between her legs to massage her heat. The fabric is damp and searing hot.

"And then I'm going to slide my cock into your sex and take you with long, hard strokes until you come."

She whimpers.

The sound of her need sends electrifying heat shooting to all parts of my body.

I dip my head and tease a nipple with the tip of my tongue and then take it between my teeth.

She cries out. I think she's trying to form words but fails. Her fingers sliding through my hair, holding me against her breast, tell me she likes what I'm doing. Likes what she's feeling. So I apply a little pressure to the bud between my teeth and tug. Her knees give way, and I steady her against me with an arm around her waist.

I move to the other breast and do the same. The sexy noises coming from the back of her throat as my tongue glides over the sensitive peak, tell me she's still all in. I back her toward the bookshelves next to the sofa so she has something to lean on.

She's going to need it.

When her ass is up against one of the shelves, I take her hand and guide it to the edge. "Hold on to this." I mold her fingers around the outer casing of the bookshelf.

She doesn't question me.

When I start kissing my way down, her head falls back and rests against a shelf. Her eyes are closed, lips parted. I feather kisses down her flat stomach and drop to my knees in front of her. I nip and bite her belly button and then whisper dirty things as I leave a bite mark on one hip.

"*Yes,*" she pants out. Her head tosses from one side to the other. "I want you, Dex. I want it all tonight."

So I start to enact all the things I've promised. I capture her panties between my teeth and tug them down. When they're mid-thigh, I pull them all the way off with one hand and toss them aside.

She's trembling even harder and spearing her fingers through my hair. "Touch me, Dex."

"Oh, I plan to, sweetheart." I bury my face in the honey-blonde triangle of curls and breathe her in. "Be patient. It'll be so much better if we take our time, I promise."

She moans and shifts impatiently, like she's both excited by drawing it out and restless to get to it. I chuckle, because that's my Ava.

I grip both of her hips and brace her in preparation for the jolt I know is coming. Then I sink my tongue into the crease between her folds and sweep across her clit.

She screams and clutches my shoulders, and I know this is going to be the best night of my life.

"That's just one flick of my tongue, Ava. You better hold on tight." I don't give her a chance to respond. I slide a hand down her thigh and place it behind a knee. Then I hook that knee over my shoulder to spread her thighs. She opens to me, and her gorgeous pussy is glistening with moisture.

I growl under my breath and delve in. Just like I did her nipples, I pull her pulsing clit between my teeth and work it.

Her cry of ecstasy rips through the room, and she writhes against me. She tastes so hot and sweet, and I love sliding my tongue into her most intimate spaces. I glance up while I'm still licking her, and she's beautiful like this. Eyes clamped shut, knuckles white where she's holding on to the shelf for dear life, the rise and fall of her chest making her full tits sway just a little. I can't wait for them to bounce wildly when she rides me at a full gallop.

She tastes as sweet and as forbidden as the cotton candy I got at the fair when I was a kid—a place my parents' said was a waste of time and intellect. But I snuck away and went instead of working on my science project. It was devilish and delicious, and I've loved cotton candy and mindless carnival rides ever since.

Ava's taste on my lips is just as decadent and delightful, and I know I'll love this even more. For the rest of my life.

Because it's forbidden. Something I'm not supposed to have, let alone enjoy.

Guilt slithers through me, but I push it out of my mind. I

can't pull away from her now. Not like this. It would crush her and make her feel less than the beautiful woman she is.

Her wetness coats my tongue as I lick and kiss. My pulse pounds through my veins and sets every nerve ending on fire. I realize I'm still dressed, and I want to strip naked and feel her soft skin slide against mine. But not yet. I don't want to stop the climax that I know is barreling toward her.

I lick and suck her clit, and find her entrance with two fingers. They slide in with no effort because she's so wet and slick. I moan against her hot pussy, and sink my fingers into her depths.

She fists my hair at the back of my head and arches into me. "*Oh God, yes.*" Her voice is a tornado of passion and need.

Her pussy is tight as I fuck her with my fingers and my mouth. She's close, I know she is, and I want to tell her to hold off. I don't because this is just the second of many orgasms I plan to deliver tonight. She can come as often as she wants. The more the better.

Her hips move with the rhythm of my tongue and fingers, and we're both so goddamn worked up and lost in the moment that nothing else matters. Just like I did on the hood of my car, I curl both fingers into her G-spot, and her climax explodes over my hand. I replace my fingers with my tongue and sink it into her wetness. It covers my lips, my cheeks. It fills my mouth, and I've never tasted anything so sinfully sweet in all my life.

Fuck cotton candy.

I kiss my way up to her mouth so she can taste herself on my lips. She molds both hands to my face and pulls me into a desperate kiss, sucking herself off my bottom lip. In-between frantic kisses, she says, "Don't make me wait anymore. Fuck me, please."

I sweep her off her feet, and she squeaks. I turn and walk down the hall.

I'm staying in Leo's old room. Uh-uh. I am *not* taking Ava to bed in that room. I'd be scarred for life. And she's staying in her parents' old master suite, so that's not an option either.

"Which is your old room?"

"Turn right at the end of the hall." Her arms are threaded around my neck. She kicks her feet up with those heels teasing me the whole way.

I reach the end of the hall, and I feel like I'm at a crossroads. My friend and business partner is to the left. Ava is to the right. A fork—each path leading to a different destiny. I hesitate and then turn right like she told me to do.

Chapter Fourteen

Ava's bedroom is still decorated for a teenage girl with ruffled curtains and boy-band posters on the walls and ceiling. It would creep me out if she weren't standing naked in front of me, so obviously a full-grown woman now.

I lay my glasses and my wallet on the white wicker nightstand that matches the headboard of her bed. I've made my choice. No idea what will happen when this weekend is over. The only thing I'm certain of is that sleeping with Ava is going to change my life even more than moving overseas.

I start to work the buttons on my vest, but her hands slide up my chest, and she takes over. One button at a time, she frees me from the vest and then starts on my shirt. I pull off the loosened tie and send it flying, my gaze never leaving her beautiful face. Her eyes are bright with fascination as the shirt falls open, and she sees my bare chest for the first time ever.

She smooths her palms over me and inhales a sharp breath when she reaches the chess piece inked over my ribcage. Her stare flies to mine, and her eyes sparkle with delight.

"My design," she says, the smile in her voice matching the one playing on her full lips. "I've never seen it on you."

I slide my shirt off. "I think of you every time I look at it," I say, and fold back the end of my belt to release the buckle. I shuck the rest of my clothes.

Ava's smoky expression tells me she likes what she sees. "Does that mean you think of me a lot?" Her fingers trace my ink. "You must look at that tat every morning when you step into the shower and every night when you get undressed."

I chuckle. "You've been in the shower with me." Like earlier tonight, for instance.

Satisfaction shimmers in her deep blue eyes. "Have I been in bed with you too?"

I growl, snake an arm around her waist, and drag her against the biggest hard-on I've ever had. She gasps, and I smother it with a punishing kiss.

"Sweetheart, you've been in bed with me every night for two solid years," I murmur against her lips.

The rise and fall of her chest causes her pebbled nipples to rub against my pecs. My cock throbs even more, and my entire body is on fire.

She pulls away just enough to slide a hand between us, and she encircles my cock. I hiss out a breath that is pure pleasure. She works my cock with her fist, up and down, up and down. She swipes the edge of one finger over my tip and uses the drop of my liquid to lube me up. Every time she reaches the base of my shaft, she flicks her wrist and pumps me again. I swear the sensation is so intense that it spreads to every cell. I've never felt anything so incredible.

So right.

"Ava," I grind out between clenched teeth. "We've both waited long enough." Two years is a long time to want someone. "It's time for me to fuck you." Because if she keeps this up, I'll come in her hand, and I want to be inside of her the first time.

She sighs against my mouth, and I walk her backwards to the edge of the bed. Gently, I lay her back, reach for a condom and cover myself, then I move on top of her. My prick is hard and hot and straining toward her.

"*Oh, God,*" she gasps when my hips settle between her legs.

"No, it's just me." I chuckle against her ear. "But I've been told it has supernatural powers."

"That's what I'm hoping for," she says and wraps her legs around my waist.

"Mmm. I like that." I nuzzle her neck, and my dick presses against her scorching hot pussy.

"So do I." Her head tips back, and she rocks into me until my tip sinks into her slickness.

I withdraw and inch into her again, teasing her entrance with the head of my dick. She bucks and strains toward me, but I keep the tease going with both my prick and my words. "How bad do you want it, Ava?" I rotate my hips so that my dick slides into her a little further, then I pull out again.

"I want it so much, Dex." Her head thrashes on the pillow. "More than I've ever wanted anything."

I love the pink flush that starts between her tits and seeps over her throat into her cheeks. I brace myself on both elbows and thread my fingers into the silky hair, framing her face. I want to remember this moment forever. The moment I first enter her all the way. I want every detail burned into my memory for all time.

I rotate my hips again and take another quick dip into her hot pussy. She moans when I pull out again.

"Rookie, open your eyes." My voice is hoarse and raw, and she does what I tell her. "Are you ready for all of it?"

She nods furiously, her breathing just as wild.

"Look at me when I fuck you, Ava. Don't take your eyes off of mine," I command.

She nods again. Our hearts pound like drums where our chests are touching. There's something so different about this moment than any other fuck I've had. *She's* different. Maybe it's our friendship. Maybe it's the bond we've developed over the years. It's like our souls are tethered and we're no longer separate beings, but she's a part of me.

Her eyes are anchored to mine. Her plump lips part, creases form across her forehead, and her creamy skin is dewy with sweat. "I want all of it. Now."

That's my Ava. She's giving me orders, and I'm happy to oblige.

I pull back and plunge into her depths with one long, lingering thrust.

She arches into me. "*Oh, Dex. God, yes.*"

I give her time to take me, adjust to me. I'm not exactly small, and I don't want to hurt her. I draw in a breath and hold it with a locked jaw. She feels so fucking good. So sweet and tight.

Her nails rake along my back until they sink into my ass. That's the signal I'm waiting for, and I start moving inside of her. I'm trying to hold back, trying to be gentle, trying to start slow and build, but that's obviously not part of Ava's plan.

Within seconds, we're fucking hard and fast, our eyes pinned to each other. I pound into her, and she meets every thrust with one of her own. Sexy little moans and sensual sounds slip through her lips as she matches me stroke for stroke, and never once does our eye contact break. We're so into each other, so fascinated with what's happening between us that nothing else exists at this moment except her and the connection between our bodies and our souls.

The creases over her brow deepen, her gaze grows more intense, and she pulls a plump lip between her teeth. I know she's close, and I dip my head to take her mouth as hard and demanding as I'm taking her sex. She kisses me back but breaks apart to stare up at me.

And I know in that moment, she wants me to see what I mean to her. How this is just a consummation of what's in her heart.

I want to tell her that I want her all to myself. I can't form the words, though, because it wouldn't be fair. Instead, I don't break my stride and fuck her harder.

She rises up so that her breasts brush my chest with each thrust of my hips. Her nails sink deeper into my ass as I drive into her.

Every muscle in my body is a fucking ball of passion and energy. I pound into her until she tightens and contracts around my dick. She cries out my name again as her first orgasm with a man inside of her crashes through her, and it's the sweetest goddamn sound I've ever heard. Her eyes slam shut, and she throws her head back, riding the wave that's cresting inside of her.

A shiver races over her as the tide of her climax finally begins to recede, and she opens her eyes.

I'm ready to go off, but I grit my teeth and hold back the riptide of orgasm threatening to send me up in flames.

Hell no. I want to see her come again.

One of my hands glides down her thigh, and I hook an arm under her knee to spread her wider. So I can reach deeper. Fuck harder.

Her eyes widen, and another spark of lust ignites in her baby blues.

"Had enough?" I ask.

She shakes her head. "I want more."

So I give it to her, riding her fast and hard.

"Dex, yes! Fuck me harder."

It's all I can do not to lose it. Gentleman that I am, I hold on and give her what she wants.

"Oh God, I'm going to come again," she says. Her eyes slide shut as her hands race up and down my back. Her bracelets jingle in my ear as her pussy closes around me, making the friction too much to bear. Her legs tighten around me, and she explodes into another orgasm. It's then I realize she's still got her heels on because they're digging into my ass. The sting of my flesh is sweet, and I can't hold back the floodgates of my own release any longer.

My dick throbs and twitches as I come.

I shower kisses over her face, her cheeks, her forehead, as our breathing slows. Gently, she traces circles along my spine with a fingernail.

"Do I still get to call you Rookie?" I murmur against her ear. "The name has kind of grown on me."

A dreamy sigh slips through her lips. "After that, you can call me whatever you want."

I'll hang on to the name. It's special, and something she and I will always share. But we both know that her rookie days are over for good.

Chapter Fifteen

I'm on my back, an arm behind my head, and Ava is curled against my side with her cheek on my shoulder. She traces circles through the smattering of dark hair on my chest.

"Which one did you have a crush on?" I'm studying the boy-band poster on the ceiling directly over her bed.

She blows out a soft chuckle and turns her head to look at the poster. "All of them." She points to the second one from the left. He's got dark features, black hair, and an overall bad-boy look. "But especially that one because he looked the most like you."

I frown at the ceiling. "I didn't know you way back then."

"Yes, you did. I'd met you once during family weekend at Columbia."

Ah. I made an effort to forget family events during those college years since my parents never showed up.

Ava snuggles into the nook of my arm, and I run my fingers through her hair.

"I hung this poster right after that," she says.

Ava's crush started that long ago?

A cold chill slithers through my veins. Could she just be infatuated with me because of Leo's overprotective sheltering? I've been convenient for her all these years. One of only two guys Leo trusts with his sister. The coldness settles into my stomach and turns it sour.

My inner geekster kicks in, and I start to analyze and intellectualize the situation. She could realize the reality isn't as good as the fantasy. When a person wants something so long, they often build it up in their minds to be much better, much bigger than it really is. I glance down at the sheet starting to tent at my crotch. Okay, I've got the bigger part handled. No problems there. But better?

No question, Ava could do better than me.

"What?" Her finger stops moving in circles, and she pokes the space between my pecs.

"*What*, what?" I ask.

"You're thinking too hard. What about?" She pokes me again.

She knows me just as well as I know her.

"I was thinking about how much history we have together. You, Leo, and Oz are the only real family I've ever known. I don't know what I'd do without you."

Her soft, pliant body stiffens at my side, and her warm flesh molded against me suddenly feels cold.

"Ava, I'm just saying I've never had this kind of bond with anyone else. Not even with my own parents, and I don't want to lose it." And it will kill me if sleeping with Ava destroys it. Even worse, if Leo finds out and goes freakazoid on us, I won't forgive myself for ruining the closeness he and Ava share.

"Let's focus on this weekend, okay?" Ava's head dips lower, and she feathers kisses down my abs.

Instinctively, my fingers thread into her silky hair. "Ava." My voice is ragged with lust.

"Mmm?" She keeps descending and moves over me. Her beautiful tits graze my abs then fall on each side of my dick.

"Fuck," I ground out.

"Uh-huh," she says, and slides her torso back and forth so that my shaft is nestled between her breasts, and they're rubbing me on both sides. And just like my fantasy, she gets me off with her beautiful breasts.

We go at it all night long, so comfortable and free with each other, like we've been a couple for years. It's even better than I'd dreamed. Everything I've ever wanted.

And so much more than I can bear to lose when this weekend

is over.

Chapter Sixteen

Morning sun streams through Ava's lacy curtains and wakes me up. I'm spooned around her with my hand cupping her breast. My ass should be dragging after our all night fuck-athon. Instead, I'm fresh as a fucking daisy and ready to go again.

But I don't make a move. I study specks of dust floating in the rays of sunlight and listen to her slow, steady breaths.

I fucked Ava.

It was so damn right and yet so wrong at the same time. After two long years of self-restraint, I've changed our friendship in one night. I've also betrayed a good friend that could blow our business partnership to hell and back. I can't even think about the implication that would have on Checkmate's future.

She stirs and snuggles closer so our bodies touch from head to toe. She wiggles her ass against my boner. "What's that?" Her voice is thick with sleep. Her eyes are closed, but a faint smile lifts the corner of her mouth.

I can't resist her, especially now that we've slept together. I don't usually spend the night with my dates. It can get awkward and harder to disengage when the relationship has run its course. But Ava isn't like any of the other women I've been with, and spending an entire night with her seems natural.

My hand closes around her perky tit, and I massage it. "It's not the Energizer bunny, sweetheart, that's for damn sure," I whisper against her ear and nuzzle her neck.

She laughs and turns her head to look up at me. She's gorgeous, messy bedhead and all.

"You're way better than the Energizer bunny." She smiles, and a sexy shade of pink seeps into her cheeks.

I slip my dick between her thighs, and it's encased in the heat from her legs, her pussy, and the bottoms of her ass cheeks.

Pure heaven.

"I'm kind of sore," she says.

Shit. I should've expected that. Instead, I was about to fuck her from behind, lying just like we are now.

She traces my jawline with her fingertips and then molds her palm to my cheek. "Last night was incredible," she whispers. "Thank you."

I resist the urge to devour her. I resist the urge to go at it fast and furious while we still can. Before the weekend is over.

I press a soft, openmouthed kiss to her lips. It's warm and languid and so, so sweet. We kiss slow and easy for a long time until our breathing starts to grow heavy. I break the kiss and brush her bottom lip with the pad of my thumb.

"I'll make us coffee while you soak in a hot bath. Maybe that'll make you feel better."

"Good idea." She rolls out of bed and takes the sheet with her, leaving me completely nude. My dick stands at attention, and her blue eyes turn to smoke and fire.

I fold both hands behind my head and let her enjoy the view. I love the way she's looking at me like she wants to eat me alive. Maybe she can later if she wants.

"What's on the agenda for today?" I ask.

"The homecoming game is tonight, so we have all day to do whatever we want." She lifts a silky brow. "I intend to make good use of our time alone together." She wraps the sheet around her and secures it above one breast.

I give her an evil smile that I hope mirrors my dirty thoughts. "Then you better soak in that hot bath a long time. With Epsom salt."

She lifts both brows and heads to the door. "That sounds like a challenge."

I push myself out of bed. "It's a promise, sweetheart."

When she's gone, I put on my glasses, find my suitcase, and

pull on a pair of sweat pants. I run a toothbrush over my grill and then pad down the hall. The wood floor is cold against my bare feet as I make my way to the kitchen. It takes a few minutes, but I find all the items I need to make coffee just the way Ava likes it. It's no surprise that she's stocked the kitchen with everything required to perform her favorite morning ritual.

It's such a *thing* for her and Leo both. Always has been since I've known them.

While it's brewing, I check my messages. I've missed calls from both Leo and Oz. Must be important. My thumb hovers over the call button next to Leo's name. Guilty SOB that I am, I can't bring myself to tap it. Mostly since I've just tapped his sister. So I dial up Oz instead.

"Hey, dude. What's up?" I grab two mugs from the cabinet.

"Uh." Oz releases a pissy breath. "I ruffled a few European feathers yesterday because of the expansion."

"Oz." My voice is stone cold. "What have you done?"

"Well, hell," he huffs. "You weren't here—"

"I've been gone one day, Oz. One. Fucking. Day."

He totally ignores me. "And Leo took a few days off to help Chloe plan their wedding, so I had to handle things myself. You know I'm not as diplomatic as you. No idea why people don't gravitate to me the way they do you and Leo."

"Maybe because you can be an asshole sometimes?" I deadpan. "Leticia has given up trying to find you an assistant because none of them last more than a few days."

"The last one stayed a week, so fuck you," says Oz. It's our standard response to each other, no matter what.

"She stayed a week because Leticia bribed her with a designer handbag and a pair of Jimmy Choos. Obviously, not even twenty-five hundred dollars of accessories made it worth her while to put up with your flowery personality, so fuck you too, buddy." I pinch the bridge of my nose. "What happened with the expansion?"

"I kind of went ape shit yesterday on the government agency in Paris that's supposed to pull the business permits for us." He hesitates. "And I may have accidentally called an official in Amsterdam an idiot." He sighs heavily. "I had no idea the Dutch speak English as good as we do."

"Jesus, Oz. Is there anyone you didn't piss off?" I ask.

"They dropped the ball, and that's no way to do business." His voice is irritated, like he can't fathom why someone didn't jump when he snapped his fingers. That's Oz.

"Their culture is just different than ours," I growl into the phone.

"It's business. How different can it be?"

"They aren't in a hurry over everything like we are. It takes patience and finesse to get things done."

"Which is why I stick to R & D and leave the ass kissing to you." Oz's sigh is heavy. "I'm not a finesse kind of guy."

"You might not suck at diplomacy quite so badly if you at least tried," I say.

"Sorry I fucked it up. I know it was already a difficult project. I turned the situation over to Leo after I lost my temper. Call him and get the rest of the deets. Meanwhile, I'll go make myself useful by developing new products that will make us millions in those European stores once they're open."

If. *If* they open. This project is already turning into one big cluster fuck, and it's just getting started.

We end the call with another *fuck you*, and I pour the coffee, mixing it up the way I do every morning at the Bump & Grind. I turn and lean against the counter, legs crossed at the ankles. I sip my coffee and pick up my phone to dial Leo. Before I can place the call, Ava emerges from the bedroom wrapped in a cozy robe that looks like it could've been her mother's. She's toweling her wet hair and smelling like the vanilla I just put in her coffee.

My thumb hovers over the call button again, and guilt skates over me.

Nope. I toss my phone onto the counter. Not gonna happen. I can't call Leo after shagging his sister. All. Night. Long.

I hand her a piping hot mug, and she brings it to her lips. "Feel better?" I ask.

She nods. "I feel fabulous." Her eyes twinkle with mischief, and she lifts her mug.

I know exactly what she'll do next. I've got it memorized after two long years of meeting her for morning coffee. Her eyes will slide shut as she sips that first taste. She'll moan, and the muscles in her neck will work as she savors and swallows....

"Mmm," she moans and her long lashes brush the creamy skin above her cheeks.

And fuck. My dick pitches a tent right inside my sweats when the lithe muscles in her neck gently roll and undulate as she swallows.

Because hey, she fucking *swallows.*

Her eyes flutter open, and she lifts the mug. "Just like my mom used to make it."

So that's why it's a *thing* for both Ava and Leo. It's a shred of their past, a part of their family tradition, like turkey cooking on Thanksgiving morning.

I realize how sad and strange it is that my parents are alive and well, yet I have not one happy memory or special family tradition to hold on to. I'm so glad that Ava does.

The mug hovers at her lips. "So I was thinking I've got a few more rookie cards I'd like to lose this weekend."

Please God, let one of them involve swallowing.

"Let's eat first, though," she says.

Eat first, swallow second. Works for me. "Eating is good." My gaze drops to the spot below the tie of her robe. "I didn't get quite enough to eat last night."

Ava snorts coffee. "Good Lord, you're a machine in bed."

I put my coffee down and walk to her. "I assure you,

sweetheart, I'm all man." I kiss her, and she tastes like cream and vanilla. "If the countless orgasms you had last night didn't prove that, I'll have to up my game."

"Are you saying my machine-made orgasms are a thing of the past?" She holds her coffee to the side so it doesn't spill.

I thread an arm around her waist. "I'm saying don't buy stock in any battery manufacturers any time soon. I've still got two days here with you."

The brightness in her eyes dims. She keeps a faint smile on her lips, but I know Ava, and it's not genuine.

"So what rookie card can I help you with today?" I try to redirect the conversation back to something that makes her eyes shine.

"Let's eat first." She backs away. "I'm starved. I think we burned more calories last night than an Olympic swimmer."

She tries to smile, but the light still doesn't return to her eyes.

Chapter Seventeen

We get dressed, and Ava directs me to a local diner where we sit on the same side of the red leather booth and snuggle like teenagers.

She leans over and nuzzles my neck, breathing in my Checkmate scent. "Sinful Obsession."

Today, I change up my usual response just a little. "Give my girl an O."

She giggles, and her eyes shine since I've called her my girl.

My phone dings again, and I look at the screen. It's Leo.

Fuck. My company could be going down the drain as we speak, and I'm too chickenshit to answer my partner's call. I can't bring myself to talk to Leo after I spent the entire night in bed with his sister. You know, the one he sent me here to look out for.

I silence the phone and stuff it back into my pocket.

The diner is teaming on a Saturday morning, and they look to be shorthanded.

"I'll be right with you," says an attractive twenty-something waitress who slows at our table with plates stacked on her arms and filling both hands. She's petite, and her wavy auburn hair is pulled back into a ponytail. She nods to the far end of the booth where the table butts against the wall. "Menus are there." She scurries off to deliver orders.

Ava watches her curiously.

When my fingers smooth over Ava's hair, she turns her attention back to me. "I was thinking I could teach you how to drive today." I tuck a lock behind her ear.

She brightens. "Another rookie card I can turn in this weekend, thanks to you."

Ava's hands are all over me under the table until Brendan,

AKA Asshat Number Two, walks in. She gets quiet and withdraws. That pisses me off because Ava never withdraws. That's what I love about her. She's never afraid to be herself. Her parents obviously cultivated that in her when she was little, and now she's a beautiful, confident woman who's comfortable in her own skin.

Brendan eyes us with disdain, last night's cheap booze reddening the whites of his eyes. There's no doubt in my mind he recognizes Ava, even though he said he didn't at the reunion. There's also no question that Ava wanted me to come here as her date for the weekend because of this asshat and his friends who haven't grown past high school.

I'm all masculine stealth and smoothness as I ease an arm around the back of the booth and stroke her shoulder. She relaxes and snuggles into me.

"Thanks," she whispers.

The blue in her eyes deepens, and I lay a lingering kiss on her lips.

The bell over the door jingles, and in walks the other member of Team Asshat. Ava stiffens when Jordan passes our booth without so much as a nod. I guess in a town this size it's hard to avoid the people you'd rather not see.

I'm rich, successful, not bad looking, and a quasi-celebrity because of Checkmate Inc. Exactly the kind of guy that intimidates the hell out of guys like Asshats One and Two, and I want them to know that Ava is beyond their reach. So I look at her like she's my queen and I'm a pawn. I worship her with my eyes, then I lean in and worship her with my tongue. Lots of tongue. And did I mention her hands? Yep, they're on the move again.

The server clears her throat, and Ava and I hit pause on the soft porn flick we're putting on in front of the entire restaurant. Ava blushes and smiles at the server. I take a quick look at the Asshat table, and my insides scream "hell yeah, we're that into each other." They're staring with their mouths open like I'm one lucky son-of-a-bitch. Because I am. I give them a quick nod. *Missed your chance, assholes. Now she's mine.*

"Have you had time to look at the menu?" The server's brow is cocked because our full attention has obviously been on each other and not today's special.

We order off the cuff, and the waitress hurries to the Asshat table. Ava keeps glancing over a shoulder to study her, so I follow her stare to see what's so interesting.

If Team Asshat hadn't already earned that title, they sure as hell do now. The two of them start billowing complaints like the customer service line on Black Friday when Best Buy runs out of wide-screens.

The waitress gives them a silent stare with a smile plastered on. She doesn't seem in the least bit rattled. I like that resilience. It takes backbone to stand up to guys like Asshats One and Two. I laugh under my breath when she licks the end of her pencil with dramatic flair and says, "What can I get you two gentlemen?"

"She looks familiar," Ava says.

The waitress walks past, grabs two waters and a pot of coffee from the drink station, and takes her time going back to the Asshat table.

While she's bent over the table to pour coffee into their mugs, Asshat One says, "If you weren't so good-looking, I'd lodge a complaint with your manager for the poor service." He's loud and obnoxious enough for most of the diner to overhear.

Asshat Two smirks.

Asshat One leers at her chest and says, "Undo another button and we just might leave you a tip." He leans in and waggles his brows. "I'll double the tip if you're a true red head." He runs a finger up her forearm.

She jerks away and splashes hot coffee all over Asshat Two.

"You cunt!" Asshat Two bolts to his feet and glares at her. "I'm gonna make sure you get fired."

My heavy training sessions at the gym kick in, and I'm out of the booth and on him before he's even able to grab for a napkin to dry his shirt. I swear, the dude has the reflexes of a sloth.

I step between the waitress and Asshat Two, grab a napkin from the table, and shove it at his chest. "I suggest the two of you leave," I say under my breath so no one can hear beyond the Asshat table. "Now."

Both Asshats sputter.

"Who the hell do you think you are?" Asshat Two huffs.

I keep my voice low and lethal. "I'm someone you don't want to fuck with. These nice folks are trying to enjoy their meals. This server is trying her best to take care of a full restaurant with not enough help." I take another napkin from the table and lean in, pretending to help him clean his shirt. "And it just so happens this has been the best morning I've ever had in my life, and you're jacking with it. So get. The fuck. Out."

I toss the saturated napkin on the table, pull myself up to my full height, and inflate my stance while staring him down with a smile.

Asshat One clears his throat. "Come on, there's better places to eat than this." He gets up. "Let's blow this pop stand."

How original.

I turn to the waitress, who is watching with a look that says, "Bring it." I want to laugh because she's five foot nothing and packed full of dynamite. Just like Ava. "Put their orders on my tab," I say to her.

When I get back to Ava, she's looking at me like I'm a hero. "That fucking rocked, you know that?" She kisses the living hell out of me.

"Damn," I say when she finally comes up for air. "I should threaten to kick ass more often."

The waitress delivers our food and says it's on the house for getting rid of the troublemakers. "Thanks." Her face is still flushed with anger from the incident.

"Their mothers obviously never taught them manners," I say.

"Do we know each other?" Ava asks. "You look familiar."

The waitress brushes off her hand on her apron and holds it out to Ava. "Kendall Tate. I was a few years older than you. I remember you and your brother."

"Well, it's good to see you," Ava says. "Sorry those guys were such jerks."

Kendall shrugs. "Occupational hazard. I'm just doing this temporarily until I can find another office job."

"You have experience as an admin assistant?" I ask. Because I happen to know a grumpy-ass partner at Checkmate who needs one.

She nods. "I had a great job, but the company made cuts." She lifts a shoulder. "I moved back here to live with my folks until I can find another job and move back to the city. There's not much selection in a town this small."

I reach for my wallet and pull out a business card. "Ask for Leticia." I hand her the card. "I'll let her know you'll be calling for a job interview."

Her face lights up. "Thank you. I...I don't know what to say."

"Don't thank me yet. You haven't met my partner, and he's the one who needs an assistant," I joke.

When Kendall goes back to waiting tables, Ava is staring at me like she wants me. I love that look, and I'm not going to make her wait for it. Even though the restaurant offered to comp our meals, I peel off two hundred dollar bills to cover our tab, the Asshats' orders, and a nice tip for the wait staff. They've earned it today.

We're barely in the car when Ava is practically straddling the console to kiss me. I drink her in, cop a feel of her fabulous rack, then pull back.

"Ready for your first driving lesson?"

"Uh-huh." She straps in and takes a gander at the bulge in

my pants. "I can't wait to work the gear shift."

The engine roars to life, and I find a secluded stretch of road to pull over. Before I can open my door to switch seats with her, she grabs my arm.

"Before you teach me to drive, I have another rookie card I want to hand over."

I pull my brows together. "What's that?"

Like a stealthy cat, she turns to face me, reaches for my pants, and has them unzipped in a second flat.

I realize she's about to go down on me right here in the car. Out in broad daylight.

And I thought I was dirty-minded.

"Ava—"

Her mouth closes around my cock, and she sucks.

"*Shit,*" I hiss out as my fingers sink into her silky hair. It falls over my lap, just like in my fantasies, and her head starts to bob. "Jesus, Ava. You're killing me."

Her blue eyes lock with mine as she keeps sucking my cock. Her magical tongue circles the head, then she licks me from tip to root.

"You deserve this for being such a hero in the diner." She plunges down on me again, applying suction.

Fireworks shoot through me and light up every nerve ending in my body. The sensation of her soft, supple mouth, tongue, and lips working my rock-hard dick is both torture and pure heaven. I close my eyes, grit my teeth, and lean my head back against the headrest.

She pumps my cock with her mouth, making sexy little noises until my skin goes from warm to surface-of-the-sun hot.

"Are you okay?" she asks, the tenor of her voice uncertain.

My eyes open to slits, and she's looking up at me, her plump, wet lips hovering just above my throbbing cock.

"Am I doing something wrong? You look...uncomfortable. Or in pain."

I laugh and frame her face with both hands. "Ava, you've got me so fucking turned on that I'm trying real hard here to make it last. It's so damn good, I don't want it to end."

She purrs. She fucking *purrs*. Then she traces the seam of her mouth with the tip of her tongue. And takes me in her mouth again. This time she goes slower. Let's the muscles in her throat relax until I'm fully encased in her wet, warm mouth.

Slowly, her tongue slides and glides up my length until she's gently holding the tip between her teeth. She breathes over me, and I shudder under the intense sensation of ecstasy racing through my veins. Gently, she molds her lips around the ridge of my tip and slides her flattened tongue over me, then she sucks me like a lollipop. When she slowly takes me all the way into her mouth again, I'm nearly hitting the back of her throat.

The faint ache of orgasm starts at my core. My muscles tense and tighten, and I let her hair slip through my fingers. I spear them in again and guide her head down to take all of me in. Instinctively, my hips start to move to match the rhythm of her mouth.

"Goddamn, Ava. It's never been this good." My voice is a growl of lust.

That seems to drive her on because she increases the pressure and the speed, fucking me with her glorious mouth as fast and hard as she can. I can't hold back any longer, and I try to pull her off me. She splays a hand on my chest to stop me cold, and keeps blowing me. The bracelets I gave her chime with each thrust, and it's playing a beautiful tune.

"Ava—" I fist her hair and try to pull out of her mouth as I start to come.

She pulls back and keeps sucking, swallowing me down.

My head falls against the headrest again, and I squeeze my eyes shut as the pure bliss of what she's doing washes through me. "I thought blowing me in a car was the rookie card you were talking about," I say between wild pants. "Apparently, I was wrong."

Thank God I was. That blow job was the sexiest thing I've ever had the pleasure of experiencing. Not to mention, this has shaped up to be the best damn driving lesson ever.

Chapter Eighteen

Let's just say Ava should stick to Uber. I'm glad we were on a deserted stretch of road in the middle of nowhere with no other vehicles...and no cliffs in sight. Plus, I may have to replace the transmission in my Porsche. I've never experienced so much grinding in my life, and not the enjoyable kind that ends in an orgasm.

We get back to her place, and spend most of the day in bed. Locking out the rest of the world, we're cocooned in this house. Lost in each other.

Until Ava finally decides it's time to get cleaned up for the homecoming game. We've been entwined with each other like pretzels all day, and I'm finally alone. In sweatpants and nothing else, I sit on the edge of Ava's bed and check my phone for the first time since Oz called this morning. It's been on silent all day, like I've gone underground.

A half-dozen missed calls from Leo pop onto the screen.

I rake a hand over my face and suddenly feel very wary.

I hang my head for a second and then pull in a weighty breath. Time to be a man and suck it up. I dial Leo.

"Hey. 'Bout time you called. I've been trying to get ahold of you all day." Leo's voice isn't as chipper as usual.

"Sorry. Your sister's kept me busy all day." I stop short. Swallow. "Uh, with homecoming stuff. Seems to be a big deal in this town."

"Yep, that's small town life. Listen, thanks again for going with her."

Leo's thanking me. For banging his sister. He may not realize it, but that's what he's doing.

I stab fingers through my bed head. "Sure, dude. Anytime."

Could I be a bigger douche?

"Oz filled you in on the latest developments overseas?" Leo's voice turns businesslike.

"Sort of. You know Oz. He said to talk to you."

"I can see why you want to be on-site. It'll be much easier to manage this project with one of us there."

Except now I don't want to leave Ava. I also can't ask her to leave her company behind in New York City. And even if I could work out the logistics of us living on two different continents, I still have no idea how Leo would react, and I absolutely cannot get between a brother and sister who have no one else in the world but each other.

That would catapult me from douche to biggest-asshole-on-the-planet. Not only would I be able to join Team Asshat, but I'd be the team captain.

"I handled it for now. Magnus and Gerard were instrumental because they know how to do business in Europe much better than we do. Let's meet tomorrow when you get back to the city. Can you guys drive home on the early side?" He chuckles. "That is if you've had your fill of fucking the hometown girls."

I freeze.

"Holy shit, man," Leo says, his voice dropping like he knows my dirty little secret.

Anger bubbles up from my stomach, and acid burns my mouth. That's not what Ava is to me. Okay, so she might be a little dirty. And fucking her is definitely a secret. But let's keep things in the proper context. She is not, nor will she ever be, a dirty secret.

"What are you talking about?" I manage to rasp out.

"You haven't seen the *City Scoop*?"

A chill slithers through my veins. "Why the hell would I read that gossip rag?"

The *City Scoop* is one of New York City's popular gossip magazines, which has had Leo, Oz, and me in their camera crosshairs since Checkmate's recent public relations scandal. Even though that mess is over and behind us, "the smokin' hot players of Checkmate Inc." still sell a lot of magazines for them. When we announced the plans to open Lifestyles Studios overseas, they shifted most of their attention to me.

Gee. I feel so fucking special.

"Chloe ran across it," Leo says.

"What the fuck does it have to do with me?" I can't mask the growing irritation in my voice.

Leo laughs. "Buddy, this morning's edition has a picture of you getting busy on the hood of your Porsche with some girl wearing a red dress sexy enough to make any man sin."

No fucking way. This is not happening.

"Shit, man." Leo barrels on. "How did you get away from Ava long enough to meet someone, much less do her in the parking lot?"

And people call *me* obtuse.

"That was kind of uncool, by the way, since you were there with my sister. I'm just glad no one thinks it was her." Leo snorts like that's the most absurd thing he's ever heard.

I rub my imploding chest. Guess it kinda feels that way when your lungs seize.

"Did it scratch the hood of your car? Because you're pretty damned OCD about that car. I'd like to meet the woman hot enough to get you to scratch up your Porsche. She must've been one epic lay."

"You...you can't tell who it is in the picture?" I can't believe I'm actually forming words.

"Nope. Her face is shadowed. Nice rack, though. Great legs too, since her dress was hiked up and they were wrapped around your waist and all." Leo spouts laughter through the phone.

I spout steam from my ears.

"It's not funny, goddamn it. Shut the fuck up, Leo." I love

him like a brother, but no one is going to talk about Ava like that. Even though he doesn't realize it's his sister he's laughing at, I still won't allow it.

"*Touchy.*" Leo tries to hide the amusement in his voice. Doesn't work. "If you don't want your sex life to go public, maybe try doing it *inside* the car next time. At least if the windows are fogged up, the photographer can't get a visual. Then you've got plausible deniability."

"Fuck you."

Leo totally ignores me. "Does Ava know you got laid in the parking lot at her homecoming reunion?"

I'm thinkin' she's pretty aware.

"If she doesn't, she will as soon as she sees that picture. Maybe give her a heads up."

I cough and pinch the bridge of my nose. Ava's gotten a heads up from me this weekend many, many times.

"I've got it handled," I say. I so fucking do not have the situation handled.

"Gotta go. The in-laws are having Chloe and me over for dinner." I hear an eye roll in his voice. "More wedding plans."

"Have fun with that."

"Chloe's going out with her sisters tomorrow night. Dinner and poker night at my place so we can talk business?"

Poker night is code for "let's play chess." The three of us came up with it after college when we traded our khaki chess team uniforms in for GQ clothes, expensive cars, and two-hundred-dollar haircuts. It's become a habit we don't care to break.

"Sure. See you then."

As soon as I end the call, I bring up the *City Scoop*. Under the Celebrity Sightings photo column, there Ava and I are, going at it on the hood of my car. It's a profile picture, but there's no doubt it's me. The only saving grace is the tree I was parked under shadowed Ava's face, concealing her identity. Her arm is looped around my neck, and my gaze settles on the gold bracelets.

The headline reads *Checkmate Inc.'s jet-setting playboy adds another notch to his designer belt*. The photo is credited to Suzanna Byers. Aka, Blondie—the soulless reporter at Ava's reunion. I wonder how much the *City Scoop* paid her for the photo. Or maybe she used it as leverage for a job. Who knows, since she obviously has no heart and no conscience?

Thank God Ava's name isn't listed as the woman I'm with. That's the way it has to stay. I've been alone my entire life. I won't be the cause of Ava losing the only family she has left.

From my phone, I fire off an email to the attorney Checkmate has on retainer. I want that reporter shut down. I tell him to threaten to sue Suzanna Byers and that smut rag for defamation. I tell him to imply that we can make serious waves for her career advancement if the identity of the woman in the picture is even hinted at. I don't care what I have to do to protect Ava.

When I'm done with my email rant, I make a promise to myself. One I don't want to make, but I've got no choice. I'll take Ava to the game. As friends. I won't hold her hand like a boyfriend should. I won't put my arm around her and pull her close like we're lovers. I won't kiss her like she's the best thing that's ever happened to me. And when the game is over and we're alone again, I won't fuck her like a man who is hopelessly hooked on her like a drug.

Instead, we'll drive back to the city tonight. I can't spend another night alone with Ava without breaking every single one of those promises.

Chapter Nineteen

After I show Ava the picture in the *City Scoop,* she wants to find Suzanna Byers. That's a mistake I can't allow to happen for Ava's own good. She's so bold and so upset that she might say something about our weekend affair that could end up in the papers again.

I assure her my attorney is handling it. Then I suggest we skip the game and head back to the city instead. The drive is tense and we're both quiet. I'm deep in thought, trying to figure out how to tell Ava that what happened upstate between us has to stay upstate. It's best for everyone if we end it now.

That's total bullshit.

It's best for her, not for me. I guess that's why I can't find a way to say the words out loud that I know will end our friendship. Losing her will cut deep.

Her scent taunts me. She smells sweet, like the grape vineyards of Tuscany during the early autumn harvest, and I want to drink her up like a fine glass of wine.

A thunderbolt of lust rockets through me when I picture Ava and me tooling through Italy together, the rolling hills on fire with the vivid colors of fall. We'd stop at a quaint vineyard for lunch. We'd meander through the rows of vines, holding hands, and we'd get caught in the rain. I'd give her a soft, sweet kiss, and she'd taste like the thunderclouds showering drops of rain down on us. We'd spend lazy days in bed, and no one would interfere in our dream world.

That really is a dream because I'll be overseas alone, and Ava will be here.

Before I know it, we emerge from the Lincoln Tunnel, and the lights of midtown Manhattan dazzle me. I gawk at them as I stop at a traffic light, waking from my dream. I'm going to miss living in this city. It's so alive, flowing with energy at any time of the day or night. The way it shifts and changes with the seasons and the time of day is fascinating.

But mostly, I'm going to miss it because this is where Ava will be, moving on with her life. Meeting other men. Dating them... probably fuc...

My brain catches fire and goes up in smoke.

Ava reaches for the stereo and turns down the music. "You've got a green light, Dex."

I'm jarred out of my daze. I bring the road ahead into focus and accelerate, shifting into second, then third. Unfortunately, my brain is still in neutral.

"Okay, tell me what's going on." Her tone is sharp and strained.

Can't say that I blame her. I want to kick my own ass all the way to New Jersey for what I've allowed to happen.

"Ava, you haven't dated much because of Leo." I want to crush the steering wheel in my hands because of what I have to say to her. "Maybe you're attracted to me because I'm around a lot. You might meet someone else while I'm away."

She pulls in a breath and looks straight ahead. "My brother has created snags in my dating life, but the truth is, I haven't tried very hard to meet other guys." Her voice goes quiet and vulnerable. "You're the one I want. I've been waiting for you to notice me. You finally did." She turns a naughty smile on me. "The picture in the *City Scoop* proves it."

I run fingers through my hair. "That fucking picture is a problem."

"My face isn't showing. Chances are no one will ever know it's me," she says. "But even if they do, I don't care. I'm glad it's me and not some other woman. The past few years, it's made me jealous when I know you've been with someone else. I've got no regrets about the picture or this weekend."

I've got plenty of regrets because it's going to change both of our lives and the comfortable friendship we've shared for so long. Yep. Definitely Captain of Team Asshat material.

I pull in a breath. "It was a great weekend." I execute each word with precision, emphasizing the last. It hangs in the air between us, and I silently run through the rest of what I have to say.

I swear, she stops breathing and stares ahead as I get closer to her apartment. Before I can finish, she says, "Pull up in front of my building. I can manage from there."

I don't pull up in front of her building like she's instructed. I will not dump her off and drive away, leaving her and her suitcases on the sidewalk like old baggage. I finally squeeze into a spot against a curb and help her with her things.

At her front door, she digs around in her gigantic purse and pulls out a ring of keys. The lock clicks, she pushes the door open, and turns to me.

"Can I come in?" I ask. We need to talk about the elephant that's filling the entire fucking building. I owe her an explanation.

She gives me a skeptical look. She's clearly pissed, and she has every right to be.

"Do you want to come in?"

Is New York City fucking crowded? Hell yes, I want to come in. I want to undress her and leave a trail of clothes all the way from the front door to the foot of her bed. Then I want to fuck her all night long, just like I did last night.

"Uh."

I have multiple degrees from Columbia. My IQ is high enough that I should have the fucking dictionary memorized, and Webster should be my bitch. *Uh* is unacceptable terminology, especially at a time like this.

I open my mouth to wax philosophical. "Uh," tumbles out again.

Goddammit.

She holds up a hand, her palm facing me. "I get it. 'It was

a great weekend,'" she mimics what I said in the car. "Now it's over."

I spear fingers through my hair, trying to find the right words. "Ava, I'm sorry. It's complicated. I don't want you to get hurt, but that's going to happen no matter how this plays out. I made a promise to your brother, and I shouldn't have let things between us get out of hand."

"I can do what I want, Dex. I'm not just Leo's kid sister anymore. I'm all grown up now." She crosses both arms under her gorgeous rack, and my mouth starts to water. I can't help but let my eyes linger over them while I think of how delicious they taste.

"Yeah, I kinda noticed the grown up part this weekend." I chuckle and stuff my hands in my pockets to keep from feeling her up right here in the hall.

"I've been waiting for you to notice for a long time." Her voice softens.

Oh, I fucking noticed long before this weekend.

"So I'm going to ask again. Do you want to come in?"

I so fucking do.

"I can't." I blow out a breath. "Ava, I owe Leo a lot..." I don't know how to finish. "There's our friendship to think about, our partnership, and Checkmate —"

The glimmer of hope in her eyes fades. "Ah," she says. "Bros before hoes."

"*No.* It's not like that." I reach for her hand.

She steps back and grasps the edge of the door. "Sure it is. You just haven't admitted it to yourself yet. The weekend's over, and we're back to our real lives. Don't worry about our coffee appointments anymore. Maybe it's time I change my morning routine."

"Ava—"

The door swings toward me and slams in my face.

Chapter Twenty

I don't sleep worth a damn all night, so I go to the gym at the ass-crack of dawn. I need a hard workout to get my head on straight before I have to meet up with Leo and Oz tonight.

I put on boxing gloves and take out my frustration on a punching bag.

I wasn't supposed to touch Ava at all, so getting the door slammed in my face after the incredible sex we had wasn't a big surprise. I might be obtuse, but even I know I deserved it. Doesn't make it suck any less, though.

A Pound of Flesh Fitness is virtually empty at this hour on a Sunday morning. Sweat flies with each blow I land to the bag. Getting in bed alone last night sucked balls. Finally having the woman I've wanted for so long only made me want her more, and it took every ounce of self-restraint I had not to run all the way back to her apartment last night, get down on my knees, beg her to forgive me for being a douche and then fuck so many orgasms out of her that it would've defied all logic and reality.

But I can't cause friction between Ava and her brother since they only have each other as family. Getting between them when I'm not going to be in New York for her would make me an even bigger douche.

Bottom line: I'm a douche either way. I should go ahead and have it tattooed on my forehead. Better yet, I should be the spokesperson for women's hygiene products with my face on the goddamn package.

Ethan Wilde, the owner of A Pound of Flesh, walks over to hold the bag for me. His dark brown hair is still damp from a shower, and he's sporting his usual five o'clock shadow. "Lot of stress?" he asks.

"You could say that." I keep on swinging.

Oz, Leo, and I met Ethan in college. He was the star of the

baseball team and headed for the Bigs until a torn rotator cuff ended his career right before he finished college. He was a jock with a flock of girls following him everywhere he went. But he was one of the good ones, and when his pro athlete dream died, he put his skills to use in a different way, just like me and my partners. Now his chain of gyms is growing with four locations in the city and more to come.

A gym membership and private training sessions are part of the five-figure package available to Checkmate clients. Our corporate agreement has helped Ethan's business grow, and we've encouraged him to try to land more corporate contracts.

"Business?" he asks as I take another swing. "A woman?"

I crush the bag with a right hook.

"Ah. A woman," Ethan says with a laugh.

I stop and take my gloves off. Ethan hands me a towel, and I wipe the dripping sweat while I try to catch my heaving breath.

"What makes you say that?" I rub the sweat off my neck.

He walks to the vending machine in the corner. "When a guy comes in here looking to destroy a punching bag, it's always because of a woman." He punches a code into the machine and brings me a bottle of water. I chug it down. "Besides, I've known you a long time, and I've never seen you like this."

True. Oz, Leo, and I were Ethan's first members when he opened. He's the one that helped us physically transform from scrawny chess team nerds to well-built men who can fill out a pair of jeans as well as any athlete. That's how our joint company venture took shape.

"First time for everything, I guess," I say.

Ethan nods. "I got fucked over once." He slices a hand through the air. "Won't happen again."

Ava didn't fuck me over. It would be so much easier if she had. Walking away from her because it's the right thing to do is the hardest damn thing I've ever had to do.

"I keep my relationships simple, 'cause I'm not giving up my bachelor status." Ethan runs a hand through the top of his hair where it's a little longer than the close-cropped sides. "Clean. Simple. No strings. I get into my bed alone every night and wake up every morning the same way. Alone."

His last word blares in my head like a fire engine. I understand "alone" all too well. I was the fucking definition of "alone" growing up. Ethan's lifestyle might've sounded convenient a few weeks ago. Now that I know how it feels to wake up with Ava's soft, naked body molded to mine, it sounds like a lonely hell.

I run the towel over my face again. My breathing has slowed, but my heart is still pounding against the walls of my chest. I shove my towel and water bottle at Ethan's chest, grab my gym bag, and head for the door.

"Thanks, man," I say to Ethan over my shoulder as I widen my strides. "That helps a lot."

"Yeah, sure," he calls after me, his forehead scrunched. "Anytime."

I don't walk; I run to the coffee shop where Ava and I have our morning coffee together. Our usual barista is there and doesn't have to wait for me to order. She starts our regulars as soon as I hit the door.

I grab two double-walled insulated mugs off the display and bring them to the cash register. "Put the coffees in these today."

Within minutes I'm hailing a cab and heading for the West Village. I'm soaking wet from my workout, but I don't care. I need to see Ava. We have a morning tradition that started with her parents, and now she and I carry it on. Maybe in a different location, and maybe in a slightly different way, but it's still our tradition. I've waited my whole life to have a family tradition, and I won't let it go without a fight.

I don't ring the buzzer at Ava's apartment. Instead, I pull out my phone and send her a text.

'Morning Rookie. Can you buzz me in before the coffee gets cold?

The dots jump, but then they stop.

Shit.

Swear to God, I'll figure out a way to climb the fire escape up to her floor with two cups of coffee in my hands if I have to.

Two twenty-something girls walk out of the front door, and I slip through. I take the stairs to her apartment two at a time, and rap a knuckle against the door while juggling the two coffee mugs.

I hear shuffling, and I know she's looking through the peephole.

Then nothing but silence.

"I'm not going away, Ava." I'll camp out in front of the door if I have to. She'll have to open the door eventually.

A loud exasperated sigh sounds through the door, and I wait for the deadbolt to slide open. It does, and there's my girl, looking sexy as hell. Tousled hair, sleepy eyes, plaid flannel pajama pants, and a T-shirt that says "Drama Queen."

Obviously, no bra, which just made my whole day.

"Can I come in?"

She holds the edge of the door with one hand. The other hand goes to her hip, and she gives me a why-the-hell-should-I-let-you-in look. "Gee, I don't know, Dex. Did you get permission from my brother?"

I deserve that. "I brought an offering." I hold up the cups.

She gives the mug a longing gaze.

I open the spout and hold it out so the aroma can work its magic.

Ava gives me a skeptical look and then her eyes trek back to the mug. Her expression doesn't soften, but she sniffs the air. "Good thing you brought coffee because your current scent isn't one of Checkmate's."

Score one for bold roasted beans. I resist the urge to smell my armpit. I guess I could've showered before I hauled ass out of the gym, but at the time, getting to Ava's door was the only thing that mattered.

She grabs the cup without a word and turns on a heel. I follow her inside and kick the door shut.

Chapter Twenty-One

Ava's bare feet shuffle along the wood floors of her apartment as she returns from the bathroom. Coffee in hand, she runs her pink tongue across pearly whites, and I know she's just brushed her teeth.

I'm still standing right where she left me, feeling awkward like I'm back in high school—a member of the chess team, trying to gain the attention of a beautiful girl. Seems hopeless.

"Sit." She points to a spot on the sofa and plops down next to it. Her braless breasts give a nice bounce, and my hand tightens around the coffee mug.

"I'm all sweaty from the gym." I discard my gym bag on the floor by the door.

"Do I look like I care?" She takes a drink of coffee. "Maybe I'll let you use my shower if you tell me why you're really here."

"I wanted to have morning coffee with you. It's what we do."

She looks as though she wants to stab me in the heart with a butter knife. Luckily, she doesn't have one handy. Still...

I take a few steps over so I'm between her and the kitchen.

"And I wanted to apologize for being a douche last night." There. I said it. "I care about you, Ava." I more than fucking care, but now isn't the right time for confessions of love. There are too many obstacles for us to overcome first.

"But what role do you want me to play in your life, Dex?" She gets that determined look in her eye. The one that has most people backing up.

The one I love and admire so much.

"Do you want me to be your sister or your fuck-fantasy?"

Okay, not admiring it quite so much at the moment. "That's...that's what I'm trying to figure out."

Her pupils darken.

"No, neither!" I sputter. "I mean, both..." Shit.

"I don't get you. You say I'm like a sister because you've known me since my parents died, we see each other every day for the last two years without you touching me, then you spend an entire night fucking me like I'm your biggest fantasy come true."

That's my girl. No holding back. Pull no punches.

Give me a hard-on with just one sentence.

Okay, her braless rack already had my hard-on well underway, but I'm splitting hairs.

"But now that we're back in the city, you're not sure what I am to you?" She runs a hand through her long waves of locks. It coasts through her fingers and falls around her shoulders. "Well, I've waited for you long enough, Dexter Moore."

Oh. Shit. When Ava calls me Dexter, it's a throw down.

"You don't get it both ways." She slaps her mug onto the coffee table and stands.

"I know how I feel about you, Ava. That's why I'm here." My mind stutters as she fingers the bottom of her shirt. "I came here to tell you that I want you. Not just for a weekend fling. I want all of you. I'm just not sure it's in your best interest."

"You have to make a choice, Dexter." With a swoosh, she pulls the shirt over her head and drops it to the floor. Both hands land on her hips, and her beautiful breasts greet me with perky nipples. "Which is it going to be—sister or lover?"

If this is her way of winning a throw down, then I don't stand a chance.

I force my gaze to meet hers. "I won't be here much the next few years."

"I don't care," she fires right back.

"Leo is a big concern for me, Ava." Goddamn gym shorts are no match for my determined prick.

"We'll figure it out." She doesn't let me off the hook. "Stop stalling." She slips both thumbs inside her pajama pants and pushes them off. "Do you want me or not?"

Holy shit. No panties. Nothing but skin. Goddamn, she's gorgeous.

And I'm toast. "Oh, I want you, Rookie." I walk toward her slowly, taking in her magnificence.

Desire flickers to life in her eyes. She steps into me, and I slide my hands around her waist. Her breasts graze my chest, and my dick strains toward her. She reaches around to hold my hands still. "I still need an answer." Her fresh minty breath washes over my jaw.

"Lover. Girlfriend. Best friend." I tighten my grip around her waist. "I want it all." I brush her bottom lip with the pad of my thumb. "We need to take it slow, though." Her lips part when I caress them. "Wait for the right time to tell Leo so he doesn't freak."

Hopefully, he *can* get used to the idea of us dating.

She lets go of my hands and slides her palms up my arms, then brushes her palm across my two-day stubble. Her eyes rake my face. "We'll tell him together."

I shake my head. "It's hard to explain, but I need to be the one to tell him."

"Why? I've never understood that weird, secret bro code the three of you seem to have."

I'm not sure I totally understand it either. We've never called it a code. "It's more like a pact that we can't put words to. It just is. I'll tell him when the time is right. Maybe we can let him get used to the idea of us dating first before he knows we're getting naked together."

She twists my shirt in both of her hands. "Speaking of getting naked. You need a shower."

I reach behind my head and one-hand my shirt. It sails across the small den.

A siren roars past her apartment building, but the sound doesn't come close to the need pounding through my veins so hard that my ears are ringing. I kiss her then, hard and hungry.

"But you can only use my shower if I get in with you," she whispers against my lips.

I slant my mouth to hers and back her toward the bathroom.

We're all over each other as we make our way into the bathroom. She turns on the shower, pulls some foil squares from a drawer, and waggles her eyebrows at me. She tosses them on a shelf next to the shower and pulls at my gym shorts. I kick them off, engulf her in my arms, and swallow her squeak with a hot kiss as I rub two fingers over her slick pussy.

"You're already wet for me," I say, then bite her bottom lip.

"I always am around you." Her head tilts to give me better access, and I blaze a trail of kisses down her neck to one plump breast. "I get wet just looking at you."

I growl and pull her into the steamy shower. The hot water rolls over us, but her skin still turns to pebbles. I lick the droplets off her neck and work my way to her ear. She nuzzles my neck and sinks her teeth in with just enough pressure to sting. I hiss in a breath when her hand closes around my cock and pumps. She reaches for a bottle of soap and pours it over me. It's not the least bit manly. It smells like flowers, but I don't give a shit. She knows I'm all man by the thick pulsing shaft in her fist.

I'm about to do the same to her when she stops me.

"Let me feel you." Her hands roam over my shoulders, lathering up the soap. She works the muscles of my chest with her fingertips and then moves to my abs. She lingers on my ink, a smile curling onto her lips.

I love the feel of her hands smoothing over me. The hot water and soap enhance the sensation even more. I'm a fucking pile of smoldering embers ready to go up in flames with one more fan of her breath.

"I want to suck your cock," she whispers.

I nearly come right then. I take her chin between my thumb and forefinger and angle her face up to mine. Our noses graze, and our breaths mingle. "That filthy mouth of yours turns me on." I kiss her hard.

She grabs my dick again and pumps fast and hard, but I stop her. I curl my fingers into her hips and turn her around. I move her hair out of the way and feather long, languid kisses over her neck. My palms start at her shoulders and coast down her arms to cover both of her hands. I guide them to the wall at the back of the shower. Then I kiss down her spine until I'm on my knees, with her sweet ass right where I want it.

I lick the inside of her thigh.

She shivers and sighs.

"That's it, sweetheart." I make sure my hot breath feathers across the sensitive lips of her pussy.

A shudder rolls over her, and she arches her back so her ass lifts toward my mouth.

I bury my face in that small crevice and tongue her.

"Oh, *God*," she gasps.

I give her wet pussy a sensual openmouthed kiss.

She moans and cusses under her breath.

I use my hands to massage up her legs, flexing my fingers into her flesh as I move up. I move my mouth to one cheek and bite the crevice where her ass meets her thigh. I nip and lick and suck every inch of her, then I do the same to the other cheek.

"I love that," she whimpers.

"I want to taste and eat every inch of you." I bite down one thigh and up the other.

"Yes," she says all breathy, like she's already close to an orgasm. I love the high tenor of her voice when she nears the edge. Her breathing gets thready, and her hips shift and quiver.

I nudge her cheeks apart with my nose and give her more tongue. And there it goes, that shimmy that tells me how much she likes what I'm doing to her. My fingers find her pulsing nub, and I work it with rhythmic strokes.

She's flooding my mouth and whimpering with need by the time I stand and reach for a condom. I can't wait another second to fuck her. When I press my rock-hard prick between her ass cheeks, she arches back against me.

"Good God, fuck me already," she rasps out.

I chuckle against her ear. "Be careful what you ask for." My voice is gritty with need.

Before she can say anything else, I dip my knees and come up inside of her with one fluid thrust.

We both moan with pleasure, and it echoes off the walls of the small bathroom.

I still, savoring the sensation of my shaft buried so completely inside of her. She wiggles her ass against my crotch, and I circle her waist with one arm to work her clit from the front. I kiss and lick the sweetness from her neck. She's still bracing herself against the wall with one hand, so I glide my other hand down her arm and lace my fingers over hers.

"I've never felt anything this good." Her voice is needy with lust.

"Me either, sweetheart." I dip my knees and fill her again.

Her head falls back against my shoulder. "You haven't?" She covers my hand with hers as I circle her pulsing nub.

I start to move inside of her and replace her fingers with mine. "Nope. Now touch yourself." I guide her fingers in circles, matching our hands with the rhythm of my hips.

"That's so naughty," she says, turning her lips to mine. "Talk dirty to me while we do it."

I laugh. My dirty talk has somehow turned to sweet words of seduction with Ava, so I dial up the dirty-word dictionary stored in my head. "I love fucking you more than anything else, sweetheart. But fucking you from behind while you fuck yourself from the front is better than any fantasy I've ever had. There are so many naughty, dirty things I want to do with you."

"Like what?" she asks. Her eyes are closed, and she's breathless.

"I want to fuck you from behind with you on all fours."

Every time I drop the F-bomb, a sexy sound slips through her lips, and I know she's getting close to the edge.

"I want you to ride my face while I fuck you with my mouth. How about sixty-nine? Or I can tie you up. Or spank this sweet ass of yours." I lean back and give her a gentle swat on the rear. She hisses in a breath. I start pumping into her again and return my lips to her ear. I rattle off a laundry list of erotic things that I'd love to do with Ava. "You name it, sweetheart, I'm game as long as you're enjoying it."

She braces herself with both hands. "Then I want it harder." She props a foot on the edge of the shower. It's like a gift.

I lean back, grasp her hips with both of my hands, and give her what she wants. We go at it until we're both worked up into a fevered frenzy. I fuck a sweet climax out of her and follow her over the edge as her velvety flesh milks a fierce orgasm from me too.

Several minutes go by as we catch our breath. She's leaning against me, all six-foot-two of me wrapped around her. She winds an arm around my neck and threads her fingers into my wet hair.

"The water's getting cold," I finally say.

"I hadn't noticed," she says. Her voice is floating and dreamy.

"That's because I'm blocking you from it."

She laughs.

We don't even bother to dry off when we step out of the shower. I lift her, and her legs encircle my waist. I carry her to her bedroom, and we spend all morning in bed. I push out thoughts of the trouble this could cause between Ava and her brother. I don't think about moving to another continent.

We work up such an appetite that Ava calls Mario's Pizza on the corner and has them deliver a large pepperoni for lunch. She says it's appropriate for the occasion. We stay in bed and eat the whole thing naked and then go at it until I finally have to call *uncle*.

The last thing I want to do is leave Ava's bed. Especially for a business meeting where I'll be making plans to leave her behind when I move. Keeping my new relationship status with Ava a secret makes guilt prickle over my spine. "I've got to meet Leo and Oz," I say as I reluctantly step into a clean pair of jeans from my gym bag.

Ava's lying face down across her bed, stark naked. She kicks one leg up and lets her hand wander up my thigh as I dig through my bag for a clean shirt. "Are you sure waiting to tell Leo about us is a good idea?"

"Hell if I know." I pull on a black T-shirt. "But blurting it out won't work either, so I think easing into it is a better plan." He never has to know that Ava was the girl on the hood of my car. Maybe if we wait a while, he won't figure that out. If we tell him now, there won't be any question in his mind that it was his sister. I'm not sure which makes me feel like a bigger asshole.

"Can you come back when you're done?" She walks two fingers up and down my thigh.

Fuck, I'm getting hard all over again. I lean down and kiss her hard. "Yes, I can come back, you naughty girl."

She shrugs. "You've created a monster, what can I say?"

"Should I bring dinner, or can I take you out?"

She lifts a brow. "Oh, you should definitely bring dinner because there's one more rookie card I want to hand over to you."

Oh, fuck yeah. This is gonna be good because there's not much we haven't already tried in the span of two days. My mind zings in a dozen dirty directions.

"Do you remember how you gave me the nickname Rookie to begin with?" she asks.

I sit on the bed next to her and pull on a sock. "Yes. You asked me to teach you chess strategy so you could beat Leo."

"Yep." She rolls onto her back, her head next to where I'm sitting. "Do you remember what you told me?"

I try to pull on the other sock, but my mind stutters to a halt when I glance at her breasts. I scan her length, and it's all I can do not to pounce like a fucking animal.

"Uh..." I'm staring at her tits, and I can barely remember my own name.

Her silky brow lifts. "If you answer my question, you can fuck them later."

I force my brain to start firing again. "I said you'd always be a rookie until you beat one of us. To my knowledge, you still haven't bested me, Oz, or Leo."

"No, but I'm going to beat *you* at a game of chess tonight."

I pull on the sock. "Really?" I cross my arms to show my skepticism. "That's a pretty cocky statement considering who you're challenging." I was one of the best during my high school and college days. Few could beat me then, and that still stands.

"First of all, the only word I just heard was 'cock.' Secondly, I've developed a strategy of my own that's sure to beat the grand master."

"You're on." I put my shoes on. "How do you intend to best a champion?" Not to be arrogant, but I'm dying to hear her answer because it's sure to be amusing.

She rises onto her elbows, and her gorgeous breasts do a bob and weave.

My eyes are fucking glued to them.

She tosses her head back and laughs. "That's how," she says with an air of confidence. "We're going to play strip chess."

Wow. Didn't see that coming. It's a chess nerd's most erotic fantasy, and she won't be the only one turning in a rookie card tonight.

"All right then." I force myself to stand before I end up burying my face between her breasts. "I'll be back later with dinner." I give her a rough, sloppy kiss. "Be ready to play. Hard."

Chapter Twenty-Two

"Checkmate," Oz says to me as he moves his rook to box in my black king for the kill.

"Shit." I cross my arms and lean back in my chair. We're sitting at Leo's dining room table, and they've both mopped the floor with me tonight. "Didn't see that coming."

Oz glances over his shoulder toward the kitchen where Leo is getting more food and beer. Then Oz leans in and whispers to me, "What the hell is up with you?"

I scrub a hand over my face. "I've got a lot on my mind tonight." Do I fucking ever. Not only do I have a sexy as hell woman waiting at her apartment to fulfill my longtime fantasy of strip chess, but Oz, Leo, and I have been discussing my imminent move overseas that will separate me from her. Just as we've finally taken our relationship to another level.

Not how I pictured things unfolding.

Oz shakes his head and starts to reset the board. "Whatever is going on started before tonight." He looks over his shoulder again. "When are you and Ava going to tell him?"

What? "Excuse me?" I feign ignorance, like I have no idea what he's talking about.

He gives me a don't-insult-my-fucking-intelligence look and crosses his arms too, like we're in a standoff.

I hang my head. There's no sense trying to deny it. The cat is so far out of the fucking bag that it's probably in Canada by now.

"How did you know?" I ask Oz.

He smirks. "Don't have to be a rocket scientist to figure it out. It's just the way you two are with each other. When Leo showed me the picture in the *City Scoop*, there was no doubt in my mind who you were with." Oz nods toward the kitchen.

"He doesn't know because he doesn't *want* to know, but it's bound to get out sooner or later. Better he hears it from you." Oz chuckles and gives me a smartass look. "Don't worry. I'll stick around and keep him from cutting off your balls."

I move my attention to Leo's large glass windows and take in the panoramic view of the city. Night has descended since it's late in the year and it gets dark earlier. Lights twinkle like diamonds scattered across a blanket of black velvet.

Leo emerges from the kitchen with a tray of chips, salsa, and beer. "Who won?"

"He did." I hitch my chin at Oz.

"You're off your game tonight, buddy." Leo digs into the chips and salsa. "Anything wrong?"

Oz gives me a shit-eating grin.

I should just spit it out. "I'm fucking your sister" would probably do the trick. Not sure even Oz could save my balls if I took that approach, though.

"Nope. I'm good." I rub my stubbled jaw. I didn't have a razor in my gym bag. Besides, Ava likes the feel of my whiskers between her thighs.

I wait for Leo to call me on my bullshit.

Instead, he says, "Okay then, let's talk business." Masterfully, that sweeps the subject under the forty-thousand-dollar Oriental rug we're sitting on. "Leticia's got your living arrangements lined up in every foreign city where we're opening a studio. I've only had to deal with the government offices responsible for pulling our business permits for one day, and I'm already worn out." Leo angles his head at Oz with a jerk. "Mr. Congeniality here has already made business enemies in at least two European countries. I definitely think you're going to have your hands full, Dex."

I nod. "That's why I need to be there. I need face time with these folks to keep the ball rolling in the right direction. It's not that they're difficult to work with. It's more about earning their trust and keeping it. We've already tied up a lot of capital in this venture, and it's only going to get more expensive before we can finally open the studios and start turning a profit to recoup those costs. The last thing we need is for them to shove us on their back burner. If I'm there in person shaking hands, wining, dining..." My words trail off. It's going be damn near impossible to be enthusiastic over this business venture that *I* wanted when all I'll be able to think about is Ava back in New York.

"If you're there in person, they're more likely to keep us on the front burner," Oz says. "And the ball stays in motion, hopefully with forward momentum that works in our favor."

"Exactly." I keep rubbing my chin. My mind keeps wandering back to a certain blonde.

"Starting Checkmate was my dream. This expansion is yours," Leo says. "We're with you all the way."

Except the expansion isn't my first priority anymore. I can't say that, though. Not after I'm the one that got my partners to sign off on this financially risky move to begin with.

"We need to get you overseas, like yesterday," Leo says. "How soon can you leave?"

The million-dollar question. The question I've been dreading. The question I don't want to answer anymore. "Next weekend." Something shifts in my chest, and a bone-deep ache rockets through me like I've just been stabbed. "That'll give me a few days to tie up some loose ends at the office."

And spend every extra minute I can with Ava, since I don't know how often we'll be able to see each other.

"Good. I'll have Leticia set up a weekly video conference between the three of us," Leo says. "I think it would be a good idea to bring Magnus and Gerard in for the calls too. They can lend some insight since they spent so much time working in the industry in Europe."

"Agreed," I say, and rub the aching spot right over my heart.

There's an expectant lull in the conversation.

"So, is there anything else we need to discuss?" Oz lifts a shoulder and stares at me. "Anything at all?"

I'm going to say it. I'm going to tell Leo how much I care for Ava, and that we're going to try to make a long distance relationship work. I'll give him my word that this isn't something I entered into without a lot of thought and assure him that I won't hurt her. I open my mouth to speak.

"Thanks again for going to Ava's reunion." Leo beats me to the punch. "I've got to loosen up when it comes to who my sister dates."

Okaaaay. Maybe this won't be so hard after all.

"But every time I look at her, I see that broken, sad teenager she was when our parents died, you know?" Leo munches on a chip. "I mean, every time I think of some guy breaking her heart, I want to toss him off of a rooftop."

Well hell. I glance out Leo's window again. It's a long way down. I didn't plan on dying today. That would make it extraordinarily hard to date Ava, regardless of the distance between us.

"Chloe says I have a double standard, and I guess she's right. When you showed up on page two of the *City Scoop* banging some girl out in public for God and everybody to see, all I said to you was 'bring it inside next time.'" Now he's smiling at me like a smartass. "But if I caught some guy disrespecting my sister on the hood of his car, I might end up doing hard time."

A text comes in, and I'm saved by the ding. Until I look at my phone, and a picture of Ava's gorgeous rack fills the screen. Her text teases me even more than the picture.

Are you hungry?

My throat closes, and I shoot both of my partners a hurried look. "Uh, I gotta go. See you guys tomorrow at the office?"

"Sure thing, man." Leo starts to clear the table like he's oblivious that anything is amiss.

Oz, on the other hand, covers his mouth with the back of his hand. I freeze, waiting for him to cough "bullshit." It's his trademark smartass comeback, and he thinks it's so damn funny. Truth is, I usually do too, until I'm the target of his smart remark. Like now.

I rub the crease of my nose with my middle finger, and Oz flashes a toothy grin at me.

I send Ava a response.

Starved. On my way.

I'll wait for a better time to tell Leo about me and Ava. I've got all of five days to find another opportunity before I leave the country. A lifetime, right?

Chapter Twenty-Three

As I leave Leo's place, I text Ava to see what she wants for dinner so I can pick it up on the way.

Her reply:

I'll order out Chinese. Come straight here.

That's my bossy girl. She knows exactly what she wants, and she's not afraid to ask for it. Even though she's waiting for me at her apartment, no doubt with multiple layers of clothes on so we can play strip chess, I'm not just thinking of shagging her again. I want to spend time with her, laugh with her. Talk, tell her stories, and I'd listen to every word of hers too.

And then, yes, I want to shag her. But more than that, I want to make love to her.

There are no taxis in sight, so I hop the subway to the village. The hustle and flow of the subway is oddly soothing. Weird, I know, but that's the way it is when you're a New Yorker. What outsiders deem as annoying chaos, a true New Yorker sees as invigorating energy.

My phone dings again, and it's Oz.

Dexter and Ava sitting in a tree. S-E-X-T-I-N-G.

I shoot a text back.

Seriously? Did your mother ask you to run away from home when you were little? Because you're one annoying SOB.

The dots jump.

Tell him, dude. Just get it over with. You're asking for trouble if you don't.

I pinch the bridge of my nose and don't reply.

When I get to Ava's apartment and she opens the door, I realize how wrong I was. Terribly, terribly wrong. Thank God.

She's not in multiple layers of clothes. She's in a silky purple robe that ties at the waist and hits her mid-thigh. It's loose at the top and parts enough to make me wonder what she's wearing underneath...if anything at all. Her shoes are the best part, though.

She turns and crooks a finger over her shoulder for me to come in and then walks to the kitchen. Her toned calves disappear into sky-high black stilettos. The robe swishes just under her ass cheeks with the sway of her hips.

"How did your business meeting go?" She starts dishing lo mein and Szechuan wontons onto two plates.

My favorites. I didn't tell her what to order; she just knew. Same as I know how to order and mix her coffee.

I shove both hands into my jacket pockets. "Uh." I'm so Goddamn articulate I amaze myself sometimes. "It went fine."

Her hand, which is dishing up our meals, slows. "What aren't you telling me?"

The pressure I'm under right now is firing at me from all angles. I feel like I'm about to crack. "Your brother doesn't know it's you in the picture." I lean a hip against the counter. "He went on about throwing a guy off the roof if they disrespected you that way."

She finishes filling our plates, grabs two beers from the fridge, and we take our dinner into the living room. Instead of eating at the small dinette table, she grabs two large overstuffed pillows from the corner and tosses them on the floor between the sofa and the coffee table. A chessboard is set and waiting in the middle of the table. We lounge on the floor next to each other and eat.

It's so natural, like we've been a couple forever. I can't enjoy it, though, because Leo's going to want to kill me when he finds out the truth.

Ava swishes her lo mein around with chopsticks. "That's why we should tell Leo together. In fact, it's probably more my responsibility than yours."

"If I were just some guy you met and started dating, I'd agree." I finish chewing a wonton and swallow. "I'm not just some guy, and if we tell him too soon, he'll know it's you in the photo." He'll go ape shit if he realizes Ava is the woman on the hood of my Porsche. I won't let Ava face that alone. I'll break the news to him first. Somehow.

She puts her sticks down and takes a drink of beer. "Maybe we could invite them to your apartment for dinner. If Chloe's there, it might help. She seems to keep him anchored when he gets..." She lifts a shoulder. "...weird."

I hadn't thought of Chloe being present when I deliver the news. Leo listens to her more than anyone else. I stab another wonton. "It would have to be this week." I put my sticks down and brush a lock of Ava's hair behind her ear. "Tonight, Oz, Leo, and I agreed that I should move next weekend."

She stops chewing, her eyes darkening with sadness...and maybe fear. At that moment, I know how unfair it is to ask her to carry on a long distance relationship for two years—maybe longer—at the same time that our relationship could drive a wedge between her and the one person in the world she counts on the most.

Her lips curve into a rigid smile. "Then eat up. We've got a game of chess to play."

"Oh, I plan to eat up, Rookie." I can't help but tease her with that nickname. She thinks she's getting rid of it tonight, but she's so not. It's going to be a helluva lot of fun watching her try, though.

We both stuff our mouths with a few more bites of food.

"So, if you win, your prize is to get rid of the nickname?"

"I thought this would be a fun way to ditch the card."

"And if I win, what do I get?" I polish off my dinner, wipe my mouth with a napkin, and toss it onto the coffee table. I don't want to think about an angry business partner, getting thrown off of a rooftop, or moving away.

She sets her plate on top of mine. "Name it."

I lift both brows because the most dirty and delicious things are running through my mind.

"Anything you want," her voice is a breathy whisper, and I know her mind is going to dirty places too.

I move to the other side of the table so I can play the black pieces. Call me crazy, but I feel more confident when I'm playing black. "Since my prize is anything I want, then I'll think about it during the match. I'm sure I can come up with something interesting." I wave to her side of the board. "Ladies first."

We take turns moving our pieces until I capture one of her knights. The piece our company logo is modeled after. The piece that's inked onto my ribcage and reminds me of Ava every time I look at it. I hold the white piece in my hand and rub it with my thumb as she slowly stands.

Her eyes never leave mine as she toys with the sash. The purple strip of silk falls through her fingers, and she slides her hand to the end to tug. The bow lets go and the robe falls open, revealing a strip of her flesh all the way down her front. I can't see her full breasts, but the valley in-between is begging to be kissed. She's got on a matching purple lace bra and panties.

Please God, let it be a thong.

With the swish of her shoulders, the silky robe floats to the floor. My throat closes. She's so fucking gorgeous standing there in sexy lace and bedroom shoes.

"While you were at your business meeting, I made a quick trip to Fifth Avenue to pick this up. Do you like it?" Her fingertip traces the top edge of her bra. With every breath she takes, her tits plump over the edge just enough to make a chess champion want to throw the match.

"Do you really have to ask?"

She blushes a little.

"Turn around and let me see the back of your panties." I'm dying to see if it's a thong.

She shakes her head. "Not until I have to take them off."

"Do I have to wait until after the match is over to fuck you?"

She puts both hands on her hips. "Unless you want to forfeit, which would make me the winner."

"Trust me, if this weren't so much damn fun, I'd consider it." But uh-uh. I've never forfeited a match. Not even in high school when I had strep. I kicked ass and went home with a purple grand champion's ribbon and slept for two straight days. That was one of the few times my parents let me miss school. And not because of strep, but because of the purple ribbon. "Make your move, Rookie."

She sits down on her pillow again and studies the board.

I am not eye-fucking her gorgeous tits. I am not picturing her bent over one of her dinette chairs while I fuck her from behind. I am all concentration and nerves of steel.

"Your turn, Dex." Her sultry voice snaps me out of my trance. "Take off your shirt."

"Huh?" I look at the board and at Ava's hand, which is holding my queen.

How did she... Wait. Oh.

She's smiling at me because she knows her strategy is working.

My eyes narrow at her as I take off my shirt. I refocus on the game.

Mostly.

I study, think, strategize. Then I make a move and capture another white piece.

Ava gets up on her knees, reaches behind her back, and unhooks her bra. Slowly, she slides the straps down each arm until her perky breasts greet me.

"It's my turn, right?" she asks, all coy and innocent.

Then she props her elbows on the edge of the table and leans forward to study the board. Her breasts hang at the most beautiful angle.

I growl.

"What was that?" She looks up at me with owlish eyes.

"You're playing dirty," I say in a gritty tone.

"Have I broken any of the rules of chess, oh, Grand Master?" she teases.

"None except indecent exposure, which is a fine rule to break from where I'm sitting." Although it's playing hell with my concentration.

She makes another move, leaning *waaaay* over the board this time. I grind my teeth into dust.

I take my time, clear my throat, then make a move. "Lose 'em." I snatch another white piece off the board.

She stands and slowly spins so that her back is to me. And good God in heaven, it *is* a thong. "I'm not sure if I want you to take those off. They're so damn sexy to look at."

"It's part of the game," she says over a shoulder as she dips her fingers into the strings around her waist and slowly lowers her panties to the ground.

Fuck, I can hardly wait to get my hands on her. And my mouth.

This time, instead of sitting back down on the floor pillow, she sits on the sofa directly in front of me. She crosses her legs and kicks up her foot, still wearing those fuck-me shoes.

"Let's see." She taps her bottom lip with an index finger. "How about this?" She uncrosses her legs, spreads them, and leans over to make her next move.

All rational thought of chess, and strategy, and winning flies out of my brain, crashes through the window, and splatters on the sidewalk below.

"Dex?" Ava slides her hands from her knees to the top of her thighs. "It's your turn."

I move a piece, but for the life of me, I have no idea which one.

"Checkmate." Ava leans over and moves her queen into place. "I win." When she tries to pick up my black king, I encircle her wrist.

"You're a very dirty girl, you know that?" I say with a growl of lust.

She shivers. "I planned to play dirty to win. And now I want you to play dirty too."

Ava just became my new favorite chess partner.

Chapter Twenty-Four

Ava and I stare at each other across the coffee table, and my fingers still encircle her wrist. We're both as still as stone statues, yet the air around us stirs with heated energy. Her eyes are mirroring what I'm certain is showing in mine. Not just lust, although it's definitely there, but a pure yearning for more than just sex.

A yearning for something deeper, like the kind of relationship her parents had. Their bond was so apparent it even showed in the pictures of them on the mantle in Weatherton.

I won't lie, though. The electrifying lust and unbelievable sex is definitely a bonus.

"You won the match, Ava," I finally say. "So you name the prize, besides loosing another rookie card."

She crooks a finger, and I come around to her side of the coffee table. She doesn't stand. Instead, she goes for my zipper.

There's no teasing, no taunting. She dives right in and takes me all the way in.

I moan, and my hips pump into her hot, wet mouth. It's an involuntary reflex because her mouth encasing my dick is like a shock of electricity to my body. She sucks me like my cock is a popsicle, the suction so fucking sweet that it's almost unbearable. Her tongue is rough, yet tender. Her lips are firm, yet soft.

She moves her mouth along my shaft, fucking me with her mouth, and I watch as my dick slides in and out. I can't take it anymore. I sink both hands into her hair and hold her head still as I move my hips instead. She cups my balls as I fuck her lovely mouth. It's the biggest fucking turn on of my life. My muscles start to tighten with the first hint of orgasm, so I pull out and grab a condom from my back pocket.

"Sit," Ava commands as I roll it on. "I'm going to ride you."

I place myself in the center of her sofa, slump down so she has complete access to my cock, and let her climb on. Just watching her move sets my skin on fire. She places my throbbing cock at her entrance and teases me by circling her hips.

I groan, curl my fingers around her hips, and slide her onto my dick. She's so wet and hot that another shockwave riots through me. We both pull in a desperate breath at the sensation of me filling her completely. I'm so deep, so fully encased by her, and it's pure ecstasy.

"Ride me, sweetheart." My voice is rough and ragged. "I want to watch you fuck me to an orgasm because it's so goddamn beautiful."

She places her hands on my shoulders, lifts herself to my tip, and sinks again. Her lips part, her skin flushes, a glistening sheen of moisture appears around her neck because she's so worked up that she's starting to sweat.

She licks her lips and keeps her eyes anchored to mine. "Can I tell you a secret?"

"'Course." We're getting too damn good at secrets, and that causes something to niggle at the back of my mind.

"I still want you to call me Rookie sometimes." She lifts again and sinks onto me, taking me in so deep that I practically see stars. The niggle is forgotten. "But I love it when you call me sweetheart, too."

Her rhythm increases, and I cover her tits with my palms. My fingers flex into them as I knead and massage them into two granite peaks. She's riding me like a naughty cowgirl now, moaning and gasping out sexy little sounds. She's hot and flushed, so her fingers slide into her own hair, and she lifts it off her shoulder in the sexiest gesture.

Her breathing becomes erratic with the first signs of the release she's searching for.

"That's it, sweetheart. Come for me. Come all over my cock." It's all hers for the taking. It belongs to no one else but Ava.

Her body starts to quiver, and she grabs onto my shoulders.

"That's it. You're at the edge." I'm not asking her. I know that she is. I've learned every signal and cue in just a few days with her. I flex my fingers into her hips again and grind into her with each of her thrusts.

"*Yes.*" Her voice is a desperate cry as her climax pulls her closer and closer to the brink.

I let my open palm glide over her flat belly into the honey-blonde triangle of curls between her legs, and I circle her throbbing clit with my thumb. That pushes her over, and she cries out my name.

I love the sound of it so fucking much that something in my chest tightens around my heart. I rise up and bury my face in the nook of her neck as I find my own release. My arms close around her tightly, and I can't imagine ever letting her go. She's become my whole world. My whole heart. My whole reason for existing.

She wraps her arms around my head and holds me just as tight. Our pounding hearts mix and mingle, and I've never felt more complete than I do at this moment.

Our friendship has grown over time, but as lovers, we're new and untested. I can only hope that how much we mean to each other can overcome all the obstacles in our path.

Chapter Twenty-Five

I'm running late Monday morning, mostly because Ava and I spent the entire night having roof-raising sex. Then I had to dart to my apartment to get cleaned up before going to the office.

As I'm about to leave my apartment, Leticia calls for a rundown of details I want her to take care of before I leave New York this coming weekend. When I hang up, I grab my jacket and head for the elevator. I send Ava a text before I step inside.

Running late. I have to skip coffee. Meet you for lunch instead?

This sucks. I've only got a few days left in the city, and skipping morning coffee with Ava is like a kick in the balls. If I can't go a day without our coffee appointment, how am I going to survive away from her for months at a time?

I nod to the doorman, pull on my wool custom cut coat, and step out into the crisp autumn air. The sidewalks of Manhattan are bustling, and a city bus roars past. A cab honks, and a traffic cop blows a whistle from the intersection just down the street.

I breathe the cool air into my lungs and look up, taking in the magnificence of this city as I button up my coat. Something washes over me. Something familiar I used to feel growing up in New Jersey. Loneliness has already started to settle into my soul, and I haven't moved yet.

My heart thuds against my chest. I don't want to go back to that dark place I grew up in, and something tells me I will when I leave this city that's become my home. When I leave my close friends that have become my family.

When I leave Ava.

I flip up my collar and start walking, bracing myself against the chill. I'm lost in thought about my future and completely forget that I should be in a hurry.

By the time I get to the Checkmate building, I'm an icicle.

The receptionist greets me and picks up the phone as I pass through the grand rotunda. No doubt, she's alerting Leticia that I've arrived so she can leap into superhero mode as she always does. That woman is amazing, and Checkmate couldn't survive without her.

As if on cue, Leticia is waiting for me when I step off the elevator. "A partners meeting is scheduled for tomorrow to discuss tightening the budget until the expansion is off the ground. Magnus is sending someone over to your apartment this week with new clothes you'll need for work and to pack all your favorites." She falls in beside me as I turn toward my office. "I've lined up only hotels with a dry cleaning and laundry service, and in the cities where I've managed to secure flats on such short notice, I've secured a valet service that will clean, stock the fridge, do laundry." She cuts a hand horizontally through the air. "Anything you need, they'll take care of it for you." She taps on the iPad that is permanently cradled in her arm. "I'm emailing the details to you now." She keeps going without taking a breath. "And Ava's waiting in your office."

Since the inside-facing walls of every floor at Checkmate are mostly glass, I know that Leo is on the phone with his feet propped on his desk. I stop and wave to him. Then I look at Leticia. "How do you do that?"

"Do what?" Her eyebrows scrunch together.

"Rule the world with a tablet and one finger," I say, and I'm totally serious.

She waggles her brows at me. "It's a really, really talented finger. Just ask my husband." She turns to stroll to her desk in front of Leo's office. "Besides, I'm Leticia. Do you not know who you're dealing with yet?"

I shake my head.

"Oh," Leticia says. "A friend of Ava's called first thing this morning. Said you gave her your card in Weatherton this weekend."

Ah. Kendall Tate from the diner.

"I've scheduled her for an interview. Good call, by the way. You need your own assistant."

"Not for me. For Oz," I say.

Leticia turns with a brow raised so high it's disappeared behind her hairline. "Does he know about this? And does she know what she's getting herself into with Oz Strong for a boss?"

I chuckle. "Better to keep both in the dark for now. At least until you see if she's right for the job."

When I get to my office, Ava is sitting on my sofa. No surprise that I find her even more gorgeous than I did last night.

The bracelets I gave her are sitting on the sofa next to her, and she's cradling her wrist.

"What happened?" I ask.

"I hurt my wrist on the way to the coffee shop this morning. It hurts like hell. There's your coffee." She nods to the to-go cup sitting on my desk.

I ignore the coffee for now. All I want is Ava. Maybe I can kiss her wrist and make it better.

"Morning." I walk to her and she stands. "Again."

She breathes me in. "Conquest." She nails my Checkmate cologne.

"Give my girl an O." I move closer and step into her personal body space without thinking. All thought of hiding our relationship is gone, and all I can focus on is that she's mine. I'm just about to dip my head and kiss her when her eyes widen, and she skitters away from me.

"Thanks for the coffee, Sis." Leo is standing in the door and lifts his cup. He eyes us. "What's going on?"

"I was just going to check Ava's wrist. She hurt it," I say.

"Are you okay?" His expression is worried.

"I'm fine." Pink seeps into her cheeks. "I just need some ice from the break room." She darts past him.

He looks at me with a grin. "Late night? You're always here early."

I shrug out of my coat and toss it on a chair. "A lot to do before this weekend."

"Leticia says everything's coming together for the move," Leo says.

"Yeah," I say. Because, you know, I'm so fucking smooth with words.

Leo keeps holding up the doorframe, drinking his coffee. He glances at my sofa, and he laugh-whispers, "Dude." He goes to my sofa and picks up Ava's bracelets. "You had the girl from the photo here last night? That's why your ass is dragging this morning?"

What the hell is he talking about? And then I remember. I fucking remember that Ava's bracelets are visible in the picture that showed up in the *City Scoop*. Yeah, *that* picture. The one of me fucking her on the hood of my car.

I haul in a breath. "Listen, there's something I need to talk to you about. Can I come over tonight?"

"Oh, thank God." Ava walks in again, a baggie filled with ice cubes on her wrist. "You have my bracelets." She goes to Leo and takes them from his hands. "I'd go ballistic if I lost them. Dex brought them to me from Dubai for my birthday."

My eyes slide shut to block out the cluster fuck that's unfolding right in front of me.

Ava's bracelets jingle.

"You sorry bastard," he says. And he's probably right.

I force myself to open my eyes and meet my best buddy's lethal stare. Force myself to watch as more than a decade of friendship and loyalty vanishes.

Chapter Twenty-Six

"What?" Ava's gaze shifts between me and Leo, confused that her brother just called me exactly what I am—a sorry bastard.

I've finally managed to live up to my parents' low expectations.

Leo's breathing is heavy, and betrayal and scorn roll off him. This guy that I've admired for having the balls to do what he wanted with his life instead of what was expected. Checkmate was his brainchild, and he cared enough about me to encourage me to follow him and his dream. So that my life would be more fun and interesting. So that I could live the adventure with him instead of being locked into the boring existence that my parents had mapped out for me. So that I could be my own person and not a robot.

I've repaid him by doing the one thing I knew would hurt him the most.

"Leo, I'm sorry," I say.

I don't think I can feel any more ashamed, but then he turns his crushing stare on his sister. My self-worth plummets like a sinkhole. The way Leo is looking at Ava tells me he'll never trust her again.

"What's there to be sorry for?" Ava asks, still not realizing we've been outed.

"*You*..." Leo runs his fingers through his hair as his stare drops to the stack of bracelets in Ava's hands. "How long have you been lying to me?"

Ava's eyes widen. "Dex told you." She looks at me. "Here? Now?"

"No, Dex didn't fucking tell me!" Leo's voice raises several notches. "I saw the picture in the *City Scoop*. The bracelets are a dead giveaway."

Leo turns his scorching gaze back on me.

The room grows hot as his laser stare burns through me. I've let my three best friends down, because not only is this going to tear apart our partnership at Checkmate, but it's also going to damage a brother and sister's bond.

I hate myself for what I've done, but I despise myself even more for what I'm about to do. My lips part as I start to stutter out an explanation. An admission of guilt that will put the blame squarely on my shoulders so Ava and Leo can hopefully find a way past this mess that I've created.

"*How long?*" Leo asks again. His voice is a whisper, but his tone is as sharp as nails.

"Just since this weekend." I'm such a damn liar. I may not have slept with Ava until this weekend, but I've been fucking her in my mind for two long years. While pretending to look out for her like a brother.

"I thought you were my friend," Leo says. So many emotions are threading through his words, none of them positive. "I trusted you to take care of my sister. I asked you to look out for her this weekend. You do that by putting her in a compromising and embarrassing position on the hood of your car, which ends up in a fucking gossip rag for all of New York City to see?"

"Leo," Ava says, and tries to lay a comforting hand on his forearm.

He jerks away from her, and her icepack falls to the floor.

"I fucked up," I blurt. "It was a mistake."

I want to close my eyes when Ava looks at me. I've just called her a fuck up. A mistake. Hurt and betrayal shimmer in her eyes, but ending our short-term love affair is the only way Leo and Ava can salvage their own relationship.

"I'm sorry, Ava." It's all I can do to look her in the eye because I know I'm driving a knife right through her tender heart. On the surface, she's tough and bold. Oh, underneath she's still strong, but she's also got a soft heart, which makes her vulnerable to people with shady intentions. That's why I understand Leo's unrelenting drive to protect her since the loss of their parents. "I shouldn't have gone with you upstate. I shouldn't have kept meeting you every morning for the past two years."

"Two years?" Leo says.

Jesus. This is such a fucking mess, but I barrel on. "I wasn't man enough to resist the temptation. I seduced her. It's all on me, Leo."

All of that is true. But I leave out the part about me also doing it because I'm in love with her. I've just been afraid to admit it to myself until now.

Ava backs toward the door, the beautiful shine I usually see in her expression completely snuffed out. She sends the stack of gold bracelets sailing across the room, and they scatter over the floor.

"You two deserve each other," she says to both Leo and me.

Leo's brows pull together. "Me? What did I do?"

"You're not a stupid person, Leo, so stop acting like it." She stops backing up and stands her ground. "I love you. You took care of me when you were little more than a kid yourself. You could've dumped me off on a relative, but you didn't. Instead, you made sacrifices for me that no one else on earth would've. But you're also suffocating me." She waves a dismissive hand in my direction, and my heart gets heavier. "You've built a shield around me by enlisting help from Dex and Oz and won't let anyone else into our world." She scoffs. "I mean, my God, Leo. This is New York City, for God's sake, and I can't get a date because you chase off every guy I meet. Then you expect me not to develop feelings for one of the only two men who meet your approval." She waves a hand in the air and then lets it slap against her side. "Why didn't you just put me in a convent? That would've been much easier for everyone. Then at least you wouldn't be so pissed at *your* friend."

She says it with so much contempt that I cringe.

She takes another step back toward the doorway, and I want to follow. I don't because I owe Leo an explanation.

She cradles her wrist again. "You can stop trying to protect me." Her stare volleys between Leo and me. "Because I've been fucked over anyway."

She turns and leaves, leaving Leo and me both locked in place. My insides turn to ice and splinter into tiny shards, the razor sharp edges slicing through me.

We're frozen in place, and if Leo doesn't go after her in the next two seconds, then I will.

Just as I'm about to move, Leo turns to me. "I want your resignation on my desk by the end of the day. I'll buy out your share of the company. I'll pay double if that's what it takes, but I want you gone."

He storms from my office and turns in the direction of the elevators, no doubt to follow his sister. I let him go so maybe they can work things out.

I'm alone in my office, staring at an empty doorway. Everything I care about has just walked through that passage. What sucks the hardest and hurts the worst is that I deserve it.

Chapter Twenty-Seven

"What the hell is going on? I could hear Leo yelling from my office." Oz screeches to a halt two steps inside my office. He scans the floor, which is still littered with Ava's bracelets. "Shit. Did Leo find out or did you and Ava break up?"

"Both." I start picking up the gold bangles.

"Shit," Oz says again, and grabs for two of the bracelets within his reach.

That has to be the understatement of the year. "No kidding." I take Ava's gifts from his outstretched hand.

"Please say you're the one that told him."

I shake my head and spin the bracelets around in my palm.

"How'd he find out?" Oz crosses his arms.

I close my fingers around the jewelry. "He recognized these from the picture in the *City Scoop*."

Oz lets a heavy sigh slip through his lips. "Shit."

Third time's a charm. I give him a look that says "Really?"

"How are you gonna fix it?" Oz asks.

"No idea other than to do what he asked and turn in my resignation." I'll gladly step aside if it means Leo and Ava can salvage their relationship. I walk around to my chair and push the intercom button. "Leticia, can you bring me a couple of boxes so I can pack up my office?" The line is thick with silence. I guess she's confused because I hadn't planned to pack a damn thing before I move overseas. We planned for everything to stay exactly as it is, so it would be waiting for me when I returned. "Leticia?"

"Um, sure," she says. "You mean for good?"

"Yes." I release the intercom button and shove the bracelets in my pocket.

"Wait a minute." Oz starts to pace. "You're quitting?"

"I don't want to, but it's best for all of us." I start to open drawers, looking for things that should go with me. "Leo doesn't want me here anymore, and it'll just hurt the company if I fight him on this."

"So you *are* quitting." Oz stops pacing, widens his stance, and stares me down.

I pull my brows together because I have no idea what he's getting at.

"I realize Checkmate was Leo's idea in the beginning, but the three of us built this company together. We'd still be manufacturing only men's cologne in fancy packages if it weren't for you. *You* came up with the idea to open retail studios. *You* developed the plan to take us global. Now you're going to walk away from all of it and leave us hanging?"

"I don't see that I have a choice."

"Of course you have a fucking choice." He starts to pace again.

Leticia walks in with two boxes. I swear that woman blinks and whatever we ask for appears. I'm certain she must live in a magic lamp. "Is there anything I can do?"

"Yes, there is," Oz says. "Get rid of the boxes. He's not going anywhere."

Leticia brightens and scurries out faster than I've ever seen her move. And that's saying something. Then she closes the door in her wake.

Oz waits until we're alone again. "Blurring the lines between business and personal seems to be a problem for both of you. Look, Leo has done his share of fucking up, or have you already forgotten?"

No, no, I haven't. "That was a little different. He wasn't banging one of our sisters."

Oz rubs his chin like he's taking that in. "You have a point."

He shrugs. "Doesn't matter, though. He still fucked up pretty bad, and did we push him out?"

I scrunch my forehead. "We kinda wanted to."

Oz angles his head and nods. "Another good point, but we didn't. We got over it and moved on. He'll get over it too."

"If I stay at Checkmate...if I stay with Ava, I'll be a constant thorn in his side. They may never patch things up."

"Of course they will," Oz says.

"You didn't see how angry he was." My chair creaks as I lean back, and I pull a cleansing breath into my lungs. I hang my head and run my fingers through my hair. Suddenly, I'm so tired.

"Didn't have to see it," Oz says. "I heard it. I think most of Manhattan heard it."

My history with Ava, Leo, Oz, and Checkmate is so intertwined that the lines are fuzzy, and I can no longer distinguish where one thing ends and the next begins. One thing is as clear as the glass walls in my office, though. Nothing is as important to me as Ava. "I hurt her. I was trying to make things right between her and Leo, but I fucked it up even worse."

Oz walks to the table in front of my sofa and picks up the black knight. Our favorite piece on the board. The one we modeled our company logo after. One hand in his pocket, he gently tosses the hand-carved knight in the air and catches it again. "Then I guess you better hurry. You've got a lot of sucking up to do to win back your woman and prove to her brother that you're the best guy for her." Oz gives me a smartass grin. The one he's so famous for. "If you start groveling now, you might be back in the Foxx siblings' good graces by Christmas so we can spend the holidays together like we always do." He tosses the piece and catches it again. "Come on, man. Don't ruin the gift exchange for me. Your presents always suck worse than mine, so I need you."

I take in what he's said, drumming my fingers against the desk. I push out of the chair. "You know what?" He's right, and I need to find her. Tell her I love her and try to rebuild the bridge between me, Ava, and Leo that I so effectively blew to holy hell and back.

"I know, I know." Oz holds a palm in the air. "I'm a fucking genius, and I've saved the day. I might as well be Superman. You can thank me later. After you go kiss ass."

I stop when I reach the door. "I was going to say that you're still an asshole, but whatever makes you feel better, dude."

Oz laughs. "Fuck you."

I smile at my buddy. "Fuck you too."

Chapter Twenty-Eight

I stop by Leticia's desk before leaving the office. "Find Leo for me, but don't tell him I'm looking for him. And have a driver meet me out front."

"Will do." She spins her chair to the side and reaches for the phone. No doubt she'll have a lock on his exact coordinates within seconds.

Sure enough, by the time I step out of the Checkmate building, my phone dings with a message from her.

At his apartment. He's waiting for me to call when you leave the building so he can come back to work. I think we're having phone trouble and my cell is about to die.

That's Leticia. She forces us to do the right thing, just like she does her own kids. I don't doubt she'd put us in timeout if she thought she could get away with it.

A black Lexus with the Checkmate logo pulls up to the curb. The driver is trained not to get out because Leo, Oz, and I don't feel comfortable with someone opening our doors for us. We've got two fucking hands, and we're not helpless just because we're successful.

I reach for the handle and pause.

I'm successful. I let the words ring in my head. I've done amazing things with my life and with my career. I thought making Checkmate a worldwide success was the answer to filling the void in my soul that's been there since I was a lonely little boy. But no. The answer is Ava. She's the only person, the only thing on earth, that makes me feel complete.

Something in my chest shifts and expands and then tightens until I can't breathe.

I pushed her away instead of fighting for her. Told her she was a mistake. A fuck up. Those words stab me in the heart like a rusty icepick.

I need to find her, ask her to give me another chance, and convince Leo that I'm the only guy that should be with his sister.

And there are snowballs in hell.

Whatever. I climb into the back seat of the car. "Leo's apartment building." I've got to give it a shot.

A decision forms in my head. I'm going after my girl. And when I find her, I'm not going to leave her behind. I'd rather give up the expansion than lose her again.

When I blow through the front door of Leo's apartment building, the doorman waves me through. I let out a sigh of relief. Thankfully, Leo hasn't already taken me off his list of visitors. When I get to his front door, I pull myself up to my full height.

I lift my hand to ring the bell, but the door swings open.

"The doorman called me," Leo says. "The big Christmas bonus I give him every year earns me some loyalty. You should try it."

I ignore the insinuation that I'm not a loyal friend. I brush past him, not waiting for an invitation to enter. "We need to talk."

"Yeah, come on in." I hear the eye roll in his voice as he shuts the door and follows me into the living room.

I stop, spin around, and stare at him. He looks normal. He sounds normal. "You're not pissed off. Why aren't you pissed off?"

"Oh, I'm pissed, buddy." Leo goes to the table and grabs his glass of OJ. "That's why I'm not offering you any." He takes a drink. "You can get your own damn orange juice."

No idea why he's not trying to kick my ass right now, but I figure this is my one shot to make things right, and I'm not going to waste it.

"Look, I know finding out about me and Ava was a shock, especially the way it happened. That picture is my fault, and I shouldn't have allowed us to be in that situation to begin with. You trusted me with your sister, and I didn't look out for her by keeping our personal business behind closed doors." I don't even pause for a breath. The words keep spewing like a broken waterline in the middle of rush hour traffic. "Leo, you're not the only one of us who doesn't have parents. And you're not the only person who loves Ava. You and Ava and Oz have been my family since I met you in college. I'd take a bullet for every one of you, but especially for Ava, because I love her more than I ever thought possible."

Leo looks past me toward the hallway. "Listen, Dex—"

"No." I shake my head. "Let me finish. I should've said this a long time ago."

He takes a drink and waves one hand for me to continue. I swear, it's like he's enjoying watching me grovel. It seems like entertainment for him.

"I've loved Ava for a long time, Leo." I rake a hand over my jaw. "And not like a sister. I *love her*, love her. As in the real deal. She's never been a mistake or one of my fuck ups. In fact, besides following you and your freakazoid dream to start this company, loving her is the smartest thing I've ever done. My only regret is that I didn't tell you myself. Now I *have* screwed everything up by telling her she was a mistake. I don't know if she'll ever give me the time of day again, but I intend to try."

"Dex—" Leo tries to interrupt me again, but I shut him down with a shut-the-fuck-up stare.

"I don't want to have to choose between loving her and having you as a friend. I don't want to have to choose between having her in my life and the company I helped you build. But if I have to, she wins. Every time. If she'll give me another chance. And you should know..." I hesitate. What I'm about to say might deal the final blow to Leo, but I know it's the right thing to do.

What the hell. I'm on a roll. "I'm not moving overseas. I can't fix my relationship with Ava if we're apart. She deserves better. I got us into this mess with the expansion, and now I'm bailing. If you want me to resign, I will. That's not what I want, but I'll do it. This expansion is going to cost Checkmate a fortune, especially if it fails. Which it might since I'm no longer moving overseas to be the watchdog."

I shove my hands in my pockets. "I'll sell my apartment. That'll bring in several million in cash, which I can put back into the business. Hell, I'll even sell my Porsche."

"Ouch." Leo puts a hand over his heart like it's been pierced with an arrow. "Not the Porsche." Then he gets serious. "You're an idiot."

So I've been told.

"The answer to this expansion has been in front of you the whole time," Leo says. "You just didn't want to see it. Oz and I weren't going to force it on you because this was your baby."

A light bulb flickers and then lights up my brain. Of course. I should've seen it sooner. "Magnus and Gerard."

Leo shrugs. "They masquerade as Europeans anyway. Might as well make it official. They can manage our overseas operations permanently." He takes a drink and studies me, a smartass smile still playing at his lips. "So you want to date my sister?"

Jesus fucking Christ. Leo takes obtuse to space station levels. "I want more than to just date her, Leo. If I can get her to speak to me again, I'm going to ask her to marry me, and I'm asking for your blessing."

Notice I didn't ask for his permission. Leo is like a brother, but it's time for him to let go of the illusion that he can protect Ava from all the risks in life. And love is a big fucking risk for anyone. I should know.

I decide it's time to dish out a little smartassery of my own. "Only because it would mean a lot to her. I actually don't give a damn if you offer your blessing or not."

"I'll tell you what." He folds an arm across his chest and steadies his glass of orange juice on top of his forearm. "If you can talk her into marrying you, then I'll freely give you my blessing."

"Really?" I'm not sure I understand, because I expected him to fight me tooth and nail.

He nods, then downs the rest of his juice. "Really." He starts toward the kitchen. "Good luck with that by the way," he says over a shoulder. "She's far more pissed at you than I am."

Okay. Not the explosive confrontation I expected. I turn to look out the expansive window when a tumble of honey-blonde hair snags my attention. I spin all the way around, and there she is. Hands on her hips.

The most beautiful woman I've ever seen. And she looks mad enough to spit nails.

Chapter Twenty-Nine

Ava's hands are firmly planted on her perfectly curved hips. I can't help but let my gaze drop to them, and I think about how much I love kissing the dip of her waist and her small, dainty hipbones.

She clears her throat. "My eyes are further north, Dexter." Her tone is harsher than ever before.

My stare anchors to hers.

Right. North.

Her foot starts tapping against the wood floors. She's wearing black leather ankle boots, and the sound echoes through Leo's apartment. She's waiting for me to fess up.

"Why didn't Leo kick my ass?" I ask. I can't help it. I need to know what's changed since I saw him an hour ago in my office.

"Leo and I have come to an understanding. Thanks to you, he realizes he can't spare me from every disappointment or the pain that life sometimes brings. It's just simply not realistic, and he's finally accepted that." She shrugs. "Or at least he's trying to. It may take some time, but I told him to suck it up and hurry the process along if he wants our brother-sister bond to continue." The speed of her tapping foot increases until it's like hummingbird wings. "Do you have something to say?"

Hell yes. There's so much I want to say right now. "Uh," tumbles out.

Goddammit.

I pinch the bridge of my nose. "I'm not sure where to begin."

"You could start with the part about loving me." A sliver of softness filters through her tone.

"I do."

She raises a silky brow. She's not letting me off that easy, and that's one of the things I love about her. She doesn't mind calling me on my bullshit.

"Love you, that is. I love you." I've never let those words form on my tongue, but I know they're true. They have been for so long. "And I'm sorry for being an ass back at my office. In my own defense, I thought I was doing the right thing for *you*. Ava, I know what it's like to be alone in the world, and I couldn't live with myself if I got between you and Leo."

"I'd be so much more alone without you, Dex." Her foot slows to a stop, and her shoulders relax. "Leo and I will work things out. So will you and Leo because that's what families do. They don't cut and run when someone disappoints them."

Mine did.

"We fight, we argue, we may even need some space from each other once in a while, but we always stick together in the end," she says.

"That's why I love you, Rookie." I take slow steps toward her until I'm standing in front of her.

Her blue eyes glitter up at me.

I take a lock of her hair between my finger and thumb and tuck it behind her ear. "So what do you say? Do you love me?"

She nods, swallowing back emotion. It's still shimmering in her baby blues, though.

"I do…" She gives me a sassy smile. "Love you, that is."

I cradle her face in my palms and slant my mouth to her exquisite mouth. She opens for me, and I slip my tongue through her lips. I kiss her long and lovingly. I want that kiss to communicate everything I feel for her.

She sighs into my mouth, and her palms slide up my chest, around my neck, and one hand weaves into my hair. Her touch sets my skin on fire, and heat rockets through me, finds its way to my heart, and encircles it.

We finally unlock our lips, and her eyes flutter open to look at me like she's floating on a dreamy cloud. "Did you have something you wanted to ask me? I distinctly remember you asking my brother for his blessing."

I drop to a knee and take her hand. "I...uh, I'm sorry I don't actually have a ring." I pull her bracelets from my pocket. "But this is the next best thing until we can go shopping tomorrow." I look up into her sparkling eyes, and I know her answer to my question before I even ask it. "Ava Foxx, will you marry me?"

"Yes." Her voice cracks, and she covers her lips with her fingertips. "Yes, I'll marry you, Dexter Moore."

I try to put the bracelets on her, but she winces.

"Sorry." She withdraws her hand.

The sting of rejection pinches my chest. She's already changed her mind.

"That's the wrist I hurt this morning." She gives me her other hand. "Put them on this one."

I crack a smile as wide as the Hudson because she's just made me the happiest man in the Big Apple. I slide the bracelets onto her wrist.

"Now get up here and kiss me." She pulls me to my feet, and I do exactly what she wants. This time, I kiss her hard and fierce to make sure we've sealed the deal.

"I'm staying in New York," I blurt. "I'm not leaving you, Rookie. Not when I've finally found you."

A breath slips through her lips that are swollen from my kiss. "So I heard. But, Dex, it's your dream."

I shake my head. "It *was* my dream. Now my dream is building a life here in New York with you."

A smile pulls at the corners of her lush mouth, and emotion brightens her eyes. "You know I'd wait for you."

"I know. But that's not the life I want for either of us." I brush the pad of my thumb over her bottom lip. I take in her beautiful face, her blue eyes, her plump lips, her slender neck.

"Eww." Leo walks in again. "Go someplace else." He plops

onto the sofa and props up his feet.

"Good idea," Ava whispers against my ear. Her hot moist breath causes a shiver to race through me.

I'd like nothing more, but I've got some unfinished business with Leo.

I squeeze Ava's side, more for my own comfort than hers. I'm not sure how to tell Leo that I've fucked up way more than anyone knows. "Truth is, the expansion is far bigger than what we can handle. Even with Magnus and Gerard overseas, the road ahead is still going to be rocky. We need more working capital than I thought."

"Which is why we've been working on a plan B." Leo laces both hands behind his head. He's drawing out the moment. He thinks it's charming and funny.

I think it's irritating.

"Wait," I say. "You two expected me to fail?"

"No, dumbass," Leo says. "We expected you to wise up like you just did and ask for help." He scoots forward until he's perched on the edge of his chair. "Let's take Checkmate public. The windfall of cash will be more than enough for the expansion."

Finally. It's all out in the open, and a million pounds of stress have lifted. I turn my attention back to the one person who deserves it the most. "Sorry I had to do this right now, but it affects your future too, so I needed to get it all off my chest before I have a heart attack at twenty-nine." I chuckle. "I'll make it up to you."

"How?" Her fingers crawl up my chest.

"Buy her a big, honkin' ring," Leo says, like he's not interrupting a thing. I take Ava's hand and lead her to the front door. "Women love that—"

The door closes behind us, blocking out Leo. I pull Ava into my arms as we wait for the elevator. "Family can be annoying," I murmur against her lips, and she giggles. "Do we really have to spend the holidays with them?" The back of my fingers smooth over her creamy cheek.

"Yes, but then we get to go home alone and get naked."

My heart skips, and my pants grow tighter. "I want that. I want it all with you. The good, the bad, and everything in-between. I especially want morning coffee with you for the rest of our lives."

"It's still morning." Her voice is breathy. "I say we go get coffee, then get naked."

"That's the best idea I've heard all day." I give her a soft, quick kiss. "Except for staying here in New York."

"Shut up and kiss me." Ava fists my shirt and pulls me in for a sloppy, wet kiss.

The elevator opens and we step in. As soon as it closes, I press a button and it freezes. We're suspended above the earth, hanging there like time is standing still for us and us alone.

At first, Ava's brows knit with confusion. But when I turn to her and she looks in my eyes, she knows what I'm about to do. A naughty smile plays at her lips.

I ease her back against the wall of the elevator, which is all mirrors. "Let me put a little cream in your coffee." I chuckle and slide my hand under her dress. "Are you attached to these leggings?"

"Not especially." Her heart is thundering where her chest touches mine.

"Good." I reach down and tear a hole right between her legs. "I'll buy you a new pair." I nip at her bottom lip. "A better pair."

She swallows and sucks in air as I press my hard-on into her.

"I'm guessing you've never done it in an elevator." I tug her panties to one side and slide a finger into her. She's already wet and throbbing, and she arches into me.

"No," she breathes out.

Within seconds I'm finger fucking her to an orgasm. "Neither have I. Another rookie card gone."

She moans and her eyes slide shut as she rides my hand, quickly exploding into a fierce climax. Her wetness fills my hand. I turn her around to face the mirror and go for my zipper. Her eyes flare when she realizes what I'm about to do, and she licks her delicious lips.

When I reach for my wallet, she shakes her head. "No condom this time."

I don't know if she's on the pill, and I don't care. I slide into her, skin on skin, and we both groan. The pleasure is almost too much to take. Fucking her bare is the best thing I've ever felt.

She braces herself against the mirrors and watches me fuck her from behind. I bend until my lips are next to her ear, but our eyes stay locked. "I want to fuck you every day for the rest of our lives." I talk dirty to her, making sure to drop the F-bomb because it turns her on.

A breath escapes through her lips, and she slides a hand over her shoulder, into my hair. My hips pick up speed until I'm fucking her hard and fast. Her skin flushes, our breathing gets hot and heavy, and we come apart together.

By the time we step into the lobby, our clothes are put together again—less one pair of black leggings. We get coffee and spend the morning in bed at her place. Then I take her shopping for a big-ass-honkin' ring, and life is good.

In fact, it's so much better than I ever thought it could be.

Epilogue

Christmas Day

"Love the new place," Chloe says when she and Leo walk in carrying an arm full of glittery presents. "It's very warm and inviting."

"It says family, doesn't it?" Ava loops her arms around my waist, and I pull her against me.

That's right. I ditched my high-brow apartment for a cozy brownstone on the Upper East Side. We've just moved in, so Ava isn't done decorating, but we went out last night and brought home our first Christmas tree. She wanted white lights. I wanted colored lights because they remind me of a county fair. We compromised and put both on the tree. Then we had incredible sex on the floor next to our work of art.

Oz walks in next with a bottle of wine and a shopping bag full of gifts. I can't wait to see what Mr. Thoughtful gives everyone this year. Last year it was flip flops and socks. No lie.

He sniffs the air. "Something smells good. I'm starved."

Ava's got a turkey cooking in the oven, and I'm making the side dishes. The aroma fills the house and my soul at the same time.

Magnus and Gerard even flew in from Europe. I'm sure the fat block of company stock they're going to get as a bonus when Checkmate goes public didn't influence their decision to accept our invitation for Christmas dinner in the least.

We sit around the long dining room table and pass dishes that are brimming with holiday food. I wanted to sit at the head of one end of the table with Ava on the other, like you see in the movies. Ava refused and claimed the chair next to me. She's talking to Magnus, who is sitting on her other side, and they're discussing drapes and linens and paint colors. Under the table she's tracing a path up and down my thigh. Silverware clinks, everyone chats, and I sit back and watch. This is my family—this wonderful, crazy band of misfits. We love each other.

Most of all, I love this woman sitting beside me. That's where I always want to be: by her side. I lift her hand to my lips and feather kisses along her fingers.

She leans in and breathes me in. Her brows pull together. "I don't recognize your cologne."

"It's a new scent I've had Oz working on. It won't hit the market until next spring." I give her a naughty caveman stare. "It's called Rookie Moves."

She returns the naughty look in spades. "I love it. It's sexy as hell."

I pick up a piece of silverware and tap it against my wine glass. Everyone quiets down, and all heads turn in my direction.

I clear my throat. Suddenly, it's closing up, and I find it hard to speak. Ava's hand closes over mine and squeezes.

"I just wanted to say thanks for letting us hold the Christmas celebration here at our new home." My voice waivers, and Ava gives my hand another squeeze. "I hope every Christmas is spent just like this...only with kids running around eventually, and maybe Oz will finally bring someone special. If he can ever find someone to put up with his grumpy-ass self."

Murmurs skitter around the table, the gist is mostly how that's entirely impossible.

He mouths "fuck you" at me from the other end of the table, and I mouth it back.

I lift my glass. "Here's to family." I bring Ava's fingers to my lips and press a kiss to them.

We all toast and knock glasses and spend the rest of the evening opening gifts by the tree.

Oz...well, let's just say he's Oz. The tacky boxers with phrases he thinks are funny written across the ass are meant with the best of intentions.

My favorite gift isn't the Italian leather jacket from Leo and Chloe. It isn't the new watch from Magnus and Gerard. Those are great and special, and I treasure both, but one gift outshines them all.

Ava hands me a larger than average gift, and I peel back the paper. I swallow back the emotion that wells up inside of me because of her thoughtfulness and the love I know she put into this present. I lock my eyes with hers. "You got me a cotton candy machine."

"You mentioned you liked cotton candy. I thought it would be fun, like our morning coffee," Ava says.

I nod and kiss her long and hard. I'm looking forward to building a lifetime full of little traditions, because to me, they're everything.

Coming Soon

Sinful Games – A Checkmate Inc. Novel (Coming Summer 2017)

Acknowledgements

As always, I owe a huge debt of gratitude to my critique partner and beta reader, Shelly Chalmers. Her input makes my prose shine. Also, I'm so lucky to have Jo Swinney and Annette Stone in my corner.

About the Author

Shelly Alexander is the author of contemporary romances that are sometimes sweet, sometimes sizzling, and always sassy. A 2014 Golden Heart® finalist, she grew up traveling the world, earned a bachelor's degree in marketing, and worked in the business world for twenty-five years. With four older brothers, she and her sister watched every Star Trek episode ever made, joined the softball team instead of ballet class, and played with G.I. Joes while the Barbie Corvette stayed tucked in the closet. When she had three sons of her own, she decided to escape her male-dominated world by reading romance novels and has been hooked ever since. Now she spends her days writing steamy contemporary romances while tending to a miniature schnauzer named Omer, a toy poodle named Mozart, and a pet boa named Zeus.

Be the first to know about Shelly's new releases, giveaways, appearances, and bonus scenes not included in her books! Sign up for her newsletter and receive VIP treatment! http://shellyalexander.net

Follow Shelly on Facebook: https://www.facebook.com/ShellyAlexanderAuthor/

Tweet to Shelly: https://twitter.com/ShellyCAlexande

Email Shelly: http://shellyalexander.net/contact/

Made in the USA
San Bernardino, CA
25 January 2017